For What It's Worth

Michael Geraghty

I0564349

Hold Fast Publishing

1

The thumping of the tire into another pothole caused Noah Healy to pry his eyes open yet again. He knew full well the view would be the same as twenty minutes prior when the tour bus rocked. Still, his eyes turned toward the small window beside his bed anyway. Darkness enveloped his view, along with the spray from the wheels, spreading snow and ice slowly as the vehicle crept along the New York State Thruway.

The band had left their last gig in Manhattan what seemed like days ago, even though it had only been five hours. When they were back in New York, the band played shows in New York City before working north to play areas like Albany, Syracuse, and Buffalo. This time was no different, and even slogging through winter weather had been commonplace over the years. However, this trip felt different. He sighed as he gazed out the fogged window and threw his head back onto the pillow, staring up at the bunk above him where his bandmate Edgar Dyer lay sleeping.

Another jolt from a pothole, more abrupt than the previous one, caused Noah to sit upright. He noticed half of Edgar's body become visible as a stray hand reached down and gripped the bunk Edgar lay on.

"Fuck, Cecil, what's going on?" Edgar snarled. "I'm gonna end up on the damn floor!"

Noah peered up the aisle to the front of the tour bus, where Cecil McAndrew, their longtime driver, worked through the messy roads.

"Sorry, Eddie," Cecil shouted back. "The road's a mess every which way, and I can barely see where I'm going at this point. This is nuts."

Noah climbed out of the bottom bunk and stood, stretching as he did after feeling cramped. The bus they used for this trip was their backup, having shelved the more luxurious transportation because it needed repairs that were outside the budget for this tour. He looked at Edgar, coming face to face with him, and smiled through the dim lighting coming from the small bulbs that lined the floor of the rig.

"This sucks, Noah," Edgar grumbled. "Explain to me why we are doing this again?"

Noah shrugged before making his way up the aisle toward the front of the bus. He moved by the two bodies using the sofa beds on either side , attempting to keep his footing so he didn't end up in the lap of either Pete Hendley, the group's bassist, or Jordan Gaspar, the guitarist, while they slept. Finally, Noah reached the front seats and moved to the unoccupied passenger seat to ride shotgun.

"I didn't mean to wake you," Cecil said to Noah as the driver focused on the road.

"No problem," Noah answered, wiping what little sleep he had from his eyes and mind. Noah glanced at the dashboard and saw it was nearly 3:00 a.m.

"Christ, we've been on the road for over five hours," Noah said aloud. "How close are we?"

"I couldn't even tell you at this point, Noah," Cecil admitted. "The snow and sleet have been coming so fast I haven't even looked at road signs or anything. I'm just trying to lock in to stay on the road. Kingston is the last sign I remember passing, but I don't know how long ago that was. Even the GPS isn't helping much. I keep losing the satellite and haven't had communication with the trailer in a while."

The bus thudded across another dip in the road, making Noah bounce in the seat. He watched as Cecil gripped the steering wheel tightly. A semi came up alongside the bus, plowing through the snow on the road and sending an avalanche of road spray onto the front window, temporarily blocking Cecil's view.

"Shit," Cecil spat out, swerving and braking at the same time. The movement of the bus proved enough to jostle the rest of the band, so groans and banging could be heard coming from the back of the bus. When the stream of expletives rang out loudly, Noah knew the ride had awakened Ray.

It wasn't long before Noah heard the telltale pounding of Ray Landry's big feet up the aisle toward the front of the bus.

"Cecil, I swear to fucking God that if you don't do something about this ride, I'm going to fire you," Ray yelled.

"I'm doing my best," Cecil answered. "There's not much I can do about it, Ray."

"Chill out, Ray." Noah intervened. He rose from his seat and put his hands on Ray's bare shoulders. "Look at the weather. It's a nightmare out there."

"I don't give a shit if he's driving through the Apocalypse," Ray replied. "I need to get some goddamn sleep."

Noah guided Ray back down the aisle as they moved past Pete and Jordan, both now awake after Ray's rants. Noah finally got Ray to the lone bedroom at the back of the bus. Ray insisted on taking it since he was the lead singer, and no one in the band wanted to deal with the confrontation if they challenged Ray.

"Just lie back down," Noah insisted. He watched as Ray sat on the spacious bed and grabbed the bottle of sleep aids he routinely kept nearby, taking several from the bottle and downing them without the help of a beverage. Noah winced as he spied Ray swallowing the pills.

"I'll fire him, I'm telling you, Noah," Ray insisted.

"Yeah, I know," Noah said with a smile, knowing full well Ray wouldn't or couldn't fire Cecil without the other band members consenting. The band had long ago written up a new contract among the members to avoid situations just like this that had become commonplace once Ray's behavior and ego had gone overboard.

Noah made sure Ray lay down on the bed before shuttering the room with the accordion door that separated it from the rest of the bus.

"Did he fire Cecil again?" Edgar asked as Noah went by.

"Almost," Noah admitted. "Go back to sleep, Eddie."

Noah returned to the front and sat down as the rest of the band resumed their attempts at slumber. He sat back and ran his hand through his brown hair before rubbing the back of his stiff neck.

"You okay?" Cecil asked as he glanced over at Noah.

"Yeah. That bunk is awful. It's too short, the padding sucks, and those pillows are the worst," Noah replied.

"Sorry, man. I know it's not like the other bus, but Jerry insisted we spend less on travel this time around. Getting it maintained and repaired just wasn't in the stars right now."

Noah thought about Jerry Martin, the group's manager that Ray had pushed onto the rest of the band a few years back. Jerry traveled by himself on this trip, trailing the tour bus and trailer in his own vehicle. He wondered how Jerry was faring on the journey, and Noah pulled his cell phone out of his pocket and dialed him.

"What's up?" Jerry said, answering immediately.

"I was just checking on you," Noah told him. "The roads are pretty bad, Jerry."

"I know. I lost sight of you guys a long time ago. I can't tell if you're ahead of me or behind me, and I have no idea where the trailer is. They aren't even answering my calls. But we'll get there eventually."

"I thought maybe we would want to get off at the next exit or rest stop and hunker down for a bit. I don't think it's safe for Cecil to keep driving."

Silence was all Noah heard on the other end after his statement.

"Jerry? You still there?"

"Yeah, I'm still here. We can't stop, Noah. We have the show in Oneonta we have to get to for tomorrow. They've sold a lot of tickets. We can't cancel and lose the revenue. I think Ray would want to—"

Noah cut Jerry off right there. "It's not just Ray's decision, Jerry."

"I get that, Noah. I really do, and I appreciate your input. But I think Ray and the rest of the band might want the paycheck instead of losing out. So why don't you let me worry about this stuff? That's my job, not yours."

I was doing just fine with it until you came along, Noah thought.

"Whatever," Noah said with resignation.

"Good," Jerry affirmed. "Now, let me get back to the road. Tell Cecil to keep moving."

Noah disconnected the call and sighed once more.

"No luck with him, huh?" Cecil commented.

"The guy's an ass," Noah said bluntly. "He wants us to keep going. I have no idea how far we are from Oneonta, Cecil. I'm sorry."

"It's not your fault," Cecil assured him. "If you don't mind keeping me company for a bit up front, it might help me. Maybe you can watch for exit signs so we can get an idea of where we are at."

"Sure, just give me one second." Noah rose from the front seat and quietly worked his way back toward his bunk, grabbing the small messenger bag he had at the foot of his bed. Noah brought the bag back with him to the front seat, buckled up, and opened the bag, taking out his worn brown leather journal. He glanced at different pages, flipping through them as he scanned remnants of lyrics Noah had abandoned before he settled on a blank page to start fresh.

"Song idea?" Cecil asked with a quick look over at Noah before turning his attention back to the snow-covered road.

"I'm not sure," Noah offered with a shake of his head. "I seem to be in a dry spell… a very long one at that."

"You'll figure it out," Cecil assured him. "You always do."

"Cecil, I haven't written an original song in years," Noah admitted. "It just hasn't been there for me. As much as Ray would like me to, I can't force it."

"Has Ray ever written any of the songs?" Cecil asked quietly, hoping to go unheard.

Noah smiled and shook his head.

"No, Ray is not the ideas man," Noah scoffed. "He's got a helluva voice and always has, but he has no sense for lyrics and music. That was always up to me… or Jack," Noah lamented.

"Sorry, I didn't mean to bring up bad memories," Cecil said.

"No, it's no big deal," Noah replied. "The band is solid with Jordan here. He's the perfect lead guitar and knows all our songs back and forth. He's just young. Christ, I can't believe how young sometimes. He makes me feel ancient at thirty."

The two men sat silently for a few minutes as Noah gazed out the foggy passenger side window. He watched as the snowflakes peppered the glass at high speed and hoped the weather and darkness might bring him some inspiration to write something new.

Cecil leaned forward to get a better view out the front windshield when he saw dimly flashing red lights up ahead of the vehicle.

"Now what?" he groused as he slowed down as they approached. Noah turned his attention to the front and saw the yellow police barriers blocking the road near the impending exit ramp. Noah rolled down his window as a man cloaked in bright yellow came up to his side of the bus.

"Hey there," the man said as he shone a flashlight brightly toward Noah, causing Noah to put his hand up to shield his eyes from the bright glow. Once Noah could focus better, he saw the signature hat of a New York State trooper.

"What's going on, Officer?" Noah asked as snow filtered in through the open window.

"Thruway is closed from here up, I'm sorry to say," the officer advised. "The drifts are too high, and the road is too slick. I just got a report of a slide of snow coming down on the road. We can't even get plows to it right now. So you're going to have to exit here."

"How far up until it opens again?" Cecil shouted over.

"It's not," the officer replied. "The governor called a state of emergency. It's closed from here to Buffalo. Wherever you're headed, you're not getting there tonight, or probably even tomorrow. The storm is a big one. My advice would be to get this thing off the road and stay somewhere safe and warm for a few days."

"Shit," Cecil muttered. "Ray and Jerry are going to have a fit."

"Are you sure there's no way around?" Noah asked. "We need to get Oneonta for a concert."

"Ha! No way. The side roads will be a nightmare," the policeman told him. "You guys in a band?"

Noah nodded, hoping he wouldn't have to go deeper into who they were.

"Yeah, we're doing a show at the university and then we're back on the road afterward.."

"Sorry I can't help you more," the cop said as he brushed snow from the brim of his hat. "Get off here and follow the road around for a few miles, and it will take you into the nearest town."

"And just where is that?" Cecil asked.

Noah watched as the officer pointed his flashlight at the exit sign. The placard was completely covered in snow. The officer trudged over, making his way through knee-deep drifts, so he could brush snow off the marker so it could be read. As soon as Noah saw the first few letters on the sign, he knew where they were.

"Emerald Lake," he uttered softly as the policeman waved his flashlight over so Cecil could direct the bus off the highway and onto the exit ramp.

2

Emma Birch sat on the small wooden bench in the mudroom. She kicked off her moccasin slippers, preparing to pull her winter boots on her feet to make the trudge to work for the evening. She had just finished tugging on the zipper when she heard the glass hit the floor in the living room, followed by the expected yelling of "Shit!" from her mother.

Emma rushed into the room to see her mother attempting to bend over from her standing position with her walker. She looked to reach for the tiny slivers of the gold glass Christmas ball that lay shattered just next to the fully decorated tree.

"Mom!" Emma yelled, causing her mother's head to snap up and look in her direction. "Leave it. I'll get it."

Emma moved to the kitchen to grab the broom and dustpan before reaching her mother's side.

"Are you trying to hurt yourself? There's no way we're getting you over to the hospital in this weather tonight."

"I was just going to move the ornament to that branch there, where it always goes," her mother insisted. Emma guided the woman back toward the recliner that sat opposite the lit tree and the television. "It didn't look right."

Emma's mother shuffled back to her seat, where Emma helped her to sit comfortably. Emma sighed before returning to where the broken glass spread out on the floor.

"Is it really that big of a deal that it was two branches off?" Emma knew as soon as the words escaped her mouth that it was, indeed, a big deal to her mother. So she prepared herself for the speech that routinely followed since she was a youngster.

"I want my tree to have a specific look to it. With all the ornaments in the right place, the tree looks impressive through the bay window, and you can catch a reflection from the fireplace. It's a small thing to ask, Emma."

Emma had mouthed all the words to herself as her mother said them before she rose from getting the last of the broken ornament. She turned toward her mother, holding the dustpan out.

"Oh, that one was one your great-grandmother had given your father and me for our first Christmas together," the older woman lamented.

"Sorry, Mom."

Emma walked off to the kitchen to dispose of the broken glass.

"Do you want some tea before I go?" Emma said, standing at the stove. She glanced up at the black-and-white cat clock on the wall, with its tail moving in rhythm as the seconds ticked by. She saw it was nearly ten-thirty, close to when she would have to leave to walk down to the Emerald Lake Hotel where she worked. But, with another winter storm raging on, even what was a five-minute walk in the summer might take her much longer.

"Don't you need to leave for work?" her mother shouted back.

"I have a few minutes to do this."

Emma placed the silver kettle over the front burner and started the gas stove. She removed the white porcelain mug with a small Christmas tree painted on it from the cupboard next to the sink. Emma marveled at the cup, another holiday treasure they had brought up from the basement just after Thanksgiving when the decorating process began.

"I can ask Hayley or your father to get it for me," her mother yelled as Emma placed the English Breakfast tea bag in the cup. Emma rolled her eyes at the suggestion.

"Dad's not home from work yet, and Hayley—well, Hayley is Hayley," Emma added more quietly, so her mother didn't hear the jab she took at her younger sister..

As the low rumble of water in the stainless steel kettle began, Emma grabbed her phone from her pocket and shot off a quick text to Hayley.

Hey – can you come down and sit with Mom? I need to leave for work.

Emma hated that she had to text to get the eighteen-year-old's attention instead of just yelling up the stairs to get her. Still, it was the only way to get Hayley's attention.

Emma took a quick scan of her phone to see any messages, almost hoping for one from her boss, Bernadette Fisher. Emma loved the idea of lounging in front of the fireplace in her PJs, listening to Christmas music, or watching *Miracle on 34th Street* (always the original, never the remakes) while sipping hot chocolate from the couch underneath one of the holiday throws that adorned the sofa.

Of course, the fantasy never came true, especially since Bernadette took over as General Manager last winter. When the Wright family owned the hotel, they lived on-site and would give Emma nights off now and then. Once they sold to the Starlight Hotel Company, all that changed. Bernadette came and started running things according to corporate policy, caring less about employees and customers. After Bernadette learned Emma was within walking distance of the hotel, she never failed to take advantage of it.

The whistling of the tea kettle grabbed Emma's attention away from her phone as she shut the gas off to silence the call. Emma poured the steaming water into the delicate cup. She placed it down on the matching saucer, dangling the tea bag on the side of the saucer so her mother could place it in the cup for just the right amount of time to steep. Emma also plucked two reindeer gingerbread cookies off the plate in the kitchen to bring along.

"I brought you a couple of cookies, too," Emma said as she put the teacup down on the side table next to the recliner. Her mother beamed up at her before gently placing her frail hand on Emma's cheek. Her mother gently brushed a few stray red hairs from in front of Emma's eyes.

"Thank you, Emma."

Emma watched as her mother dunked the teabag and then bit off the frosted antlers of one of the cookies.

The bounding and thumping down the wooden stairs behind her caused Emma to spin around. She saw Hayley, dressed in a tank top and pair of bike shorts, entering the living room with her phone in front of her face.

"What's up?" Hayley asked, not even looking up as she typed and smiled.

"Can you sit with Mom for a bit? I need to go, and Dad isn't home from the shop yet."

"Does she really need me down here? I was just about to do a call with a bunch of my friends."

"Can you two not talk about me like I'm not even in the room, please?" their mother interjected. "I'm not an invalid."

"Mom, not to be mean or anything, but you are an invalid. You're not strong enough to do things for yourself. So Hayley can put off a call with the Gigglers until Dad gets here and keep you company."

"Hey! Don't call them that!" Hayley stated, placing her hands on her hips.

Emma sighed and eye-rolled before bending down to kiss her mother on the cheek.

"Got your phone?" Emma asked her mother.

"Right here in my robe pocket," her mother answered. "Call me when you're on your way home."

"I don't want to wake you."

"You won't. I want to know when to expect you," her mother replied.

Emma knew arguing would be futile and nodded. She grabbed Hayley's hand and dragged her sister into the kitchen and back to the mudroom. She pulled her jacket off its customary hook and put it on while facing her sister.

"Don't just go back upstairs after I leave, even if Mom tells you that you can," Emma asked, trying not to sound annoyed.

"You know she will," Hayley said as she handed Emma the red wool scarf hanging on the next hook. "She's just going to doze off in the chair once her tea is done. She won't even talk to me while I'm down here."

"That's not the point, Hayley," Emma said as she grabbed her red wool hat. "She shouldn't be by herself. If Mom tries to get up or something, she could fall. She's not strong enough to do stuff for herself. Besides, you can always talk to her, you know. You only have a few more months until you'll graduate and be off to college. So take advantage of the time you have with her. Dad will be here soon. He probably got stuck with everyone picking up Christmas stuff and then supplies to wait out the storm. You know him. He won't leave until the last customer got what they needed."

"Okay," Hayley groaned. "But I'm not watching *It's a Wonderful Life* with her again or listening to that Johnny Matthews record—"

"Johnny Mathis." Emma laughed. "It's her favorite Christmas album."

"Whatever it is, I can't do it again."

"Play cards with her. She'll love that," Emma suggested as she pulled her black leather gloves on.

Hayley nodded and gave her sister a hug.

"See you later," Emma said as she opened the back door.

A slight drift of snow had already piled up on the back steps she had swept off an hour ago. She carefully walked down the stone stairs, holding the steel railing her father had put in at springtime when her mother first got home from the hospital.

Emma shuffled through the snow on the walkway that led to the driveway. She didn't even bother with her car on days like this. Cleaning it off, shoveling the driveway, and then maneuvering down the road, even though it was a short ride, would all still take longer than the walk. Just as she waded through the last of the snow on the driveway and turned into what she assumed was where the sidewalk was, headlights shone in her direction. Emma watched as the plow blade on the front of her father's truck lowered and pushed snow in the driveway forward to clear a space.

Clay Birch lumbered out of his pickup. He slammed the truck door, causing some snow built up on the doors and tires to fall off.

"You leavin' already?" Clay asked.

"Dad, I have to be there in twenty minutes. So you're pretty late tonight."

"Sorry, honey. You know how it is this time of year. The holidays are creeping up on us, and then with this storm, everyone who didn't have shovels, rock salt, or anything else came in and wiped me out. I even sold the last two generators I had in the store. I had to help Roger Erickson load one in his truck before I could leave. Everything okay inside?"

Emma pulled down her scarf slightly, so her mouth became visible.

"Yeah, Mom's settled in now. I made her some tea. She tried to move some ornaments and broke one. I cleaned it up."

"Your motherand that tree," Clay answered, shaking his head. "If it's not perfect, it will keep her up at night. Do you want me to give you a ride? It's pretty rough tonight."

"You know I love to walk in the snow." Emma smiled.
"Since you were a toddler." Clay laughed. "Once you were moving, it's all you wanted to do in the winter. Just be careful. There's no one out on the roads, but things are slippery."

"Go inside, Dad," Emma insisted before hugging her father and turning back to the sidewalk.

The only sounds Emma heard on her walk were the wind whipping by and her feet crunching the snow beneath her. She would occasionally kick up the snow in front of her as she moved along the dimly lit street until she reached Main Street. The street glowed from the hanging Christmas lights strung above the road. She moved past The Birch Tree, her family's general store that held the prestigious spot on the corner at the start of Main Street. She gazed into the front windows with the ornate Christmas scenes and designs she had helped her father with since she was a preteen, noticing the tiny ski lift still running its miniature skiers up to the top of the snow-covered mountain where the lodge rested.

Emma hurried along, skirting past the front door of The Hidden Jewel Pub and then the Emerald Diner, the only two businesses still open at this hour and in the current weather. She gave a casual wave to Pauline McGraw, visible through the diner window, as she poured coffee for the lone patron seated at the counter. Emma secretly hoped the diner would be open when she left the hotel in the morning to grab a breakfast sandwich on her way home.

Emma reached the front of the Emerald Lake Hotel. Those on the previous shift had cleared most of the snow from the front sidewalk and sprinkled a liberal amount of rock salt to prevent icy spots that might form from the inevitable drip of melting snow and ice that would occur from the eaves of the hotel. She knew that she or Tony Baldwin, the overnight maintenance worker, would be shoveling the walk several times during the night.

Emma pulled on the front door and found it locked. She looked puzzled since the doors were not supposed to be closed until midnight. She peered through the glass and knocked, hoping to get the attention of Marianne Bailey, the front desk clerk who worked the shift just before Emma's. When Marianne didn't appear, Emma used her teeth to pull the glove off her left hand so she could rap loudly on the glass.

As she moved her legs up and down, the cold coming through the black dress pants she wore, she spotted Tony pushing a mop and bucket across the lobby floor. She knocked quickly to get his attention and waved to him. Tony hustled over to unlock the door.

"Sorry, Emma," the older man noted. "I didn't hear you out there."

"No problem," Emma said as she began to take off her winter gear. "Why is the door locked? Where's Marianne?"

"She didn't come in. Her car didn't start, and Gary is out of town on an overnight haul to Maryland."

"Who's been running the desk?" Emma asked as she got closer to the desk, carefully stepping across the newly-cleaned marble floor in the lobby.

"Guess," Tony grumbled under his breath as his head pointed toward the office door behind the counter.

"Oh no." Emma sighed.

Emma hung up her coat on the coat rack in the corner. She removed her boots and slipped into the black flats she always wore at work, then straightened her crisp white blouse before putting on her Emerald Lake Hotel name tag that read Emma Birch, Night Manager. She tied her red hair back into a ponytail when she heard Bernadette's voice bellow over the radio Tony had clipped to his hip.

"Tony, is Emma here yet?" Bernadette's raspy voice crackled.

"Good luck," Tony said softly as he scurried off toward the elevators.

Emma knocked on the closed office door twice before entering the room. Bernadette sat at the desk, the position she always took up. Her salt-and-pepper hair was in a tight bun and gave her the stern schoolmarm look all the employees secretly compared her to. Emma always thought Bernadette looked more like the Wicked Witch of the West, even right down to the cackling laugh Bernadette broke out when she did succumb to laughter.

"Hey there," Emma said as cheerfully as she could. Bernadette eventually looked up from the computer screen to see Emma.

"Finally," she said with exasperation.

Emma glanced down at her watch, noting that she was still ten minutes early for the night shift.

"Technically, I don't start for another ten minutes," Emma began.

"I know," Bernadette said with condescension dripping in her voice. "But you're always early. It's been such a long day. I can't believe Marianne called out. It's unacceptable."

"Well, if she's having car trouble, and Gary isn't around, there really is no way for her to get here, especially in this weather," Emma replied. "They live up on Skyline, and that hill is—"

"I don't care about that," Bernadette shot back. "She has a job to do, and she should be here. I really should write her up with corporate, leaving me like that."

"I don't think that's necessary," Emma added softly, not wanting to rile up Bernadette further. "Was it hectic today? I didn't think we had a lot of reservations on the books. How many rooms are in use?"

Bernadette glanced at her computer screen.

"Four," she mumbled.

Emma knew two had come in the previous night, which meant they only had two new visitors all day. She did her best to stifle a laugh in front of Bernadette.

"Anyway, now that you're here, you can take over," Bernadette said gruffly as she grabbed her purse from the bottom drawer of the desk. "All the occupied rooms are on the first floor, so the top two are unoccupied. I need you to restock the supply pantry for the guests and stop giving away things like toothpaste or deodorant. Guests are supposed to get charged for those amenities. That's why we have the pantry there."

Emma followed Bernadette out of the office and watched as the older woman grabbed her black overcoat and put it on.

"I'll get right to that," Emma noted as she walked toward the large Christmas tree so she could plug the lights in.

"What are you doing?" Bernadette asked as she buttoned her coat.

"I was going to plug in the tree," Emma said as she bent down.

"Don't do that," Bernadette ordered. "There's no one here, and likely not to be anyone here with this weather. So we don't need it on. It's a waste of electricity. Goodness knows our expenses are high enough."

"But I'm here," Emma said softly.

"Really, Emma," Bernadette replied. "If you ever want to be a general manager of a hotel, you have to learn what's essential and watch the bottom line. These little frivolous things add up. Didn't they teach you that at Oneonta? I can get you the manager training books Starlight gives out in their program. You'll learn just what to do to be successful."

Bernadette made her way across the marble floor, her heels sliding on a damp spot so that she scuffled and stumbled but held her balance. All Emma could picture was a Tom and Jerry cartoon where Tom slides in place across a wet floor, and she did all she could to keep from breaking out in laughter.

"Jesus!" Bernadette shouted. "And get Tony out here to dry this damn floor! Don't let him just sit around all night in the maintenance room watching TV."

"Got it," Emma said, giving a thumbs-up.

She watched as Bernadette left the building and walked to the right to head to the side of the building where the parking lot was located. As soon as she saw the black BMW drive past the front hotel windows, Emma plugged the Christmas tree in and dimmed the lobby lights, letting the glow of the multicolored bulbs fill the room. Next, Emma went behind the counter and turned on the stream of

Christmas music. Johnny Mathis was singing, "I'll be Home for Christmas," and Emma grinned. She grabbed the Santa hat she had in her bag and put it on before dancing her way over to the coffee station in the lobby to make a fresh pot for what she hoped would not be a long night.

3

The bus bounced around as Cecil drove along slowly, watching every curve and bend in the road carefully for fear of slipping off and ending up in a ditch or ravine. The winding streets had few, if any, streetlights, with only the bus's headlights and distant lights from one of the few houses dotting the wooded areas along this stretch to Emerald Lake. Noah kept a close watch on where they went to help Cecil as much as he could.

"Christ, this is horrible," Cecil grumbled. "How do people around here get any place in the snow?"

"They're used to it," Noah added. "Getting snow up this way is just part of life. You learn how to drive in it safely from the beginning. There's a twist in the road coming up about a hundred feet from here you'll want to slow down for."

Cecil eased his foot off the barely-pressed gas pedal to slow down further without stepping on the brakes.

"How did you know that?"

"I spent some time here when I was younger," Noah admitted. "I went to school at Oneonta for a couple of years before the band took off. My roommate was from Emerald Lake."

"So you know where we're going?" Cecil breathed a bit easier. "Any idea where a hotel might be?"

"There was a Holiday Inn just up the road here on the right before you get into the town," Noah answered as he pointed.

"I only see darkness and woods."

"Yeah, there's plenty of each around here," Noah replied.

The bus reached a straight corridor after the twists and turns, revealing some scattered streetlights along the way to give some guidance. Noah glanced at one lamp and saw nothing but white streaks coming down through the cascading light.

"It should be close," Noah added, looking intently out the window. The bus slowed down, and Noah rolled down his window a bit to get a better look. The Holiday Inn sign was there, but it wasn't lit at all. Instead, the hotel lay dormant, with the entranceway to the property covered in deeper snow. Cecil stopped the bus just outside the entrance to the parking lot.

"I think we're out of luck," Cecil bemoaned. "It looks like they went out of business a while back. When was the last time you were here?"

"I don't know... maybe ten years ago. I was nineteen, I think. Sorry, Cecil."

"Well, let's hope they have something else farther on in town. I don't know how much longer I can drive without getting us stuck in the snow."

Cecil pulled the bus back onto the slick roadway and inched along the road as Noah looked for anything he might recognize. But, unfortunately, the weather, the night, and the years that had passed all made it exceedingly difficult to jar any memories, other than his thoughts of Paul Birch, his roommate at Oneonta. It was only when he noticed the sign welcoming drivers to Emerald Lake that he had any hint of recognition of the location.

"We should start seeing some signs of life now," Noah said as he sat back in the passenger seat and gazed out the window.

"Thank God," Cecil muttered. "I don't suppose there are any fast-food joints around here to grab food?"

"There weren't when I came here," Noah stated. "They had a diner, a pub, and a Chinese food place, and that was it. Nothing will be open right now anyway."

Noah watched as the bus pulled past the property on the right side of the road that he remembered most. The yard and front of the house glowed with Christmas lights and decorations, just like he recalled when Paul had brought him home on winter break from college. The tree inside framed the bay window perfectly at the front of the house. A quick glance up at the Colonial's top floor showed only light in one of the three windows, with the center, where Paul's room was, dark. Noah reflexively slumped back in his chair and shifted his eyes forward.

The bus crept into the quiet town with no signs of life at 4:00 a.m. Snow blanketed the roads and sidewalks, appearing untouched by human life. Noah craned his neck forward before pointing to the right side of the street.

"Up there," Noah indicated. "That was the only other hotel around here."

Cecil peered through the snow just coming off the front window so he could spot the sign for the Emerald Lake Hotel.

"It's going to have to do," Cecil said as he parked the bus directly in front of hotel entrance. He left the engine running while he opened the door to the tour bus and hopped out. Noah watched as the burly man walked gingerly toward the hotel doors to avoid falling. He saw Cecil tug on the door several times without it opening. Noah tensed, almost hoping no one would come to the door or buzz Cecil in so they could leave town and go somewhere else.

Cecil turned back toward the bus, shrugging his shoulders in defeat. He took two steps back toward the bus before Noah saw him abruptly turn back to the door. Cecil tugged the door open and entered the hotel while Noah sat in silence.

Maybe they have no rooms available, Noah thought. *Christmas is just three days away. They could be full.*

Noah tried not to look at the hotel doors and stared straight ahead, watching the rhythmic movement of the wipers work feverishly to clear the fast-falling snow from the glass. Then, the touch on Noah's shoulders caused him to jump in his seat. He turned quickly and saw Edgar standing by his side.

"What's going on?" Edgar asked.

"Cecil is trying to get us rooms here," Noah answered passively.

"Good," Edgar replied. "I need a real bed to sleep in for a change and a shower that might actually have hot water. Should I go wake the guys?"

"I'd wait. They might not have anything available."

Noah realized he had a bit too much hope in his voice that the hotel might not have any vacancies.

"You okay, man?" Edgar asked.

"Yeah, just really tired," Noah told him. He shut the journal that lay open on his lap before Edgar could get a close look at it.

"Come up with anything?" Edgar said, nodding toward the book.

"Nah, not really," Noah acknowledged. Then he spotted Cecil coming back to the bus, causing his stomach to tighten.

"They've got rooms for us." Cecil smiled. "Why don't you guys go grab your bags and get out. They told me I could park the bus in the lot at the back of the building."

Edgar dashed back down the aisle, awakening the bandmates to the news before heading back toward where Ray slept to rouse him.

Noah sighed and rose from his seat to go back to his bunk area. He grabbed the duffel bag he kept stored beneath his bunk, tucked the journal into it, and went to get off the bus. He reached for his black leather jacket and put it on, knowing the weather would jolt him as soon as he exited the bus.

The cold robbed Noah's breath as soon as he stepped outside. He avoided the puddle of slush just beyond the bus's last step and leaped onto the sidewalk. He stepped under the awning for the hotel for some cover from the snow and wind and heard the rock salt crunch beneath his feet. It wasn't long before the other band members were joining him in the same spot.

"Where the fuck are we?" Pete asked, wiping sleep from his eyes.

"A little town called Emerald Lake," Noah said as he watched Pete light a cigarette. "We're still a bit away from Oneonta."

"Jeez, this place is like walking into the Andy Griffith Show," Pete answered as he looked around.

"What's that?" Jordan added as he slipped his hooded sweatshirt on.

"Shit, I forget how young you are." Pete laughed. "It's a TV show from the sixties. You know, what you refer to as olden times. It was a small-town place just like this. Get used to small towns, kid. It's kind of our thing now."

Edgar jumped off the bus with his bag, rolling his eyes.

"His highness is giving Cecil a hard time about putting clothes on," Edgar told Noah.

"Do you want me to go in there?" Noah asked.

"Nah, Cecil's got him jeans at least. It'll just be a minute."

The quartet stood around before Ray finally made an appearance on the bus steps. Noah watched as Ray looked around, unsure of where he was before stepping off the bus and right into the snow and slush.

"Fuck!" Ray yelled. "These are eight-hundred-dollar leather boots. They're going to pay for a new pair. This should have been cleared before I got off the bus."

Noah stood back and shook his head as Cecil came up behind Ray and guided him onto the sidewalk. Cecil carried Ray's bag and led the way inside the hotel, where the others followed behind. Noah made sure to bring up the rear and stay behind the group.

Cecil moved across the marble floor to the front desk, with Ray trailing right behind him. Noah had never stayed in this hotel the times he came to Emerald Lake, always staying with Paul at his home when he visited, at the insistence of Paul's family. He turned to his right and saw the fireplace roaring, with several red velvet high back chairs positioned around it. He and Edgar walked over to the chairs to gain some added warmth.

"Seems like a nice place," Edgar hinted as he looked around. "It's clean, kinda homey. It's got to be way more comfortable than some of the dumps we've stayed in over the years, huh, brother?"

Noah nodded silently as he sat down on the soft cushions, running his hand over the velvet arms of the chair. The seat alone was more comfortable than his bunk on the bus, and Noah felt he could just sleep right there.

"That's the truth," Noah answered softly.

Noah turned as he heard raised voices coming from the front desk area. Pete slowly made his way over to where Noah and Edgar sat around the fire. Pete positioned himself with his back to the flames to look at his bandmates.

"What's going on?" Edgar asked.

"Ray being Ray," Pete huffed. "He's bitching at the girl behind the desk about everything. His boots are wet, there's no one to take his luggage, there's no restaurant at the hotel for his breakfast, they don't have any suites he can use... the usual prima donna stuff he spews. But I give the girl credit. She's handling him like a pro."

"Don't you know who I am?" Ray's voice boomed, echoing throughout the lobby.

Noah realized that was the sign for him to get up and try to help Cecil before Ray got them booted out of the only spot within miles for them to rest right now.

Before Noah did, Pete and Edgar reached the front desk, stepping in front of Ray to help calm the situation.

"She hasn't even fuckin' heard of us," Ray lashed out. "Let's go somewhere else where we will at least get some respect."

"I know, it's a real travesty, Ray," Noah said calmly. "Unfortunately, there is nowhere else for us to go unless you want to sleep on the bus."

"It's bullshit, man," Ray yelled. "They have no suites at all. Just rooms with king or queen beds. And they don't have a restaurant or bar. I need my breakfast, bottles of water, a drink now and then. This isn't going to work. Where's Jerry?"

"Jerry is God knows where right now," Noah responded. "Ray, it's probably just for one night. We can make do and see how things are in the morning... Christ, it already is practically morning. Let's just get some sleep, okay?"

The disgust was evident on Ray's face, but he nodded anyway. Noah gave a thumbs-up sign to Cecil, who continued on with the hotel arrangements. Pete, Edgar, and Jordan eventually migrated over to where Noah and Ray stood once they saw the tirade had ended.

"It will be nice to have a real bed," Pete offered as he stretched his back.

Cecil approached the group, holding the card keys in his right hand.

"Okay, we're all on the top floor," Cecil said as he passed out the cards. "We're lucky. They gave us each individual rooms since each room up there only has one bed in it, and she gave me a break on the price. Typically checkout is at twelve, but the girl offered us a late checkout at three tomorrow since they aren't real busy."

"What a shock," Ray interjected. "This place looks like it hasn't been updated since the sixties."

"She's doing us a favor, Ray," Noah added.

"Whatever," Ray said, waving his hand. "Cecil, bring my bag up. I'm going to my room." Ray had already begun to take his shirt off by the time he reached the elevators.

"I have to go move the bus," Cecil remarked.

"I'll get his bag," Jordan said, grabbing the heavy suitcase. Pete, Jordan, and Edgar all moved to catch the elevator while Noah stayed with Cecil.

"You need any help?" Noah asked his friend.

"Nah, I'm good. I'll go park the bus and grab my bag and lock up. Go get some sleep."

Noah watched as Cecil ran back out to the bus, and he took the slow turn toward the front desk. He walked over, intent on apologizing to the front desk clerk for Ray's behavior and thanking her for her Herculean efforts.

As he approached, he saw the strands of red hair peeking out from beneath the Santa hat the woman wore. She was tall and lithe, and Noah heard the rapid click of the computer keyboard as she worked.

"Hey, I just wanted to say thanks for helping us out, and I'm sorry for my friend's behavior. Unfortunately, he can be something of a jerk."

"Oh, it's no trouble at all," the woman said happily. "I'm glad to help."

When she glanced up from the keyboard, Noah caught the look in the hazel eyes staring back at him. A glint of recognition crossed his mind, and his eyes shot over to the name tag pinned to her white blouse so he could confirm his suspicions—Emma Birch, Night Manager.

Emma smiled at him cordially, waiting out the awkward silence that now hung in the air.

"Sir?" she asked. "Are you okay?"

"Twig?" Noah questioned and her smile faded once she recognized Noah.

4

Few people ever referred to Emma as 'Twig,' and certainly, no one since Paul was around. Yet, as soon as she heard the words leave the stranger's mouth, her smile turned to a look of concern. Emma studied the face in front of her, unsure of who she saw at first. The beard and short hairstyle threw her a bit, but something about the way he stood, the way his eyes shone at her, gave Emma the glint of recognition she needed.

"Noah?" she said softly.

Noah nodded silently, and a hint of a smile crossed his lips. It was the smile that confirmed it for her. Noah's smile always made Emma melt. As a lovesick teenager, she became elated when she knew her older brother was bringing his college roommate home. Even if it was just for a day, Emma felt excitement. She spent extra time cleaning her room, made sure she had something she thought was pretty to wear, and even went the extra mile to make breakfast or snacks when Noah was around. While Paul may have treated her like the kid sister she was sometimes, Noah always smiled, was kind, and took an interest in what she had to say—or at least it seemed that way to Emma.

"What are you doing here?" Emma said, snapping out of her mini-trance.

"The weather forced us off the Thruway," Noah explained. "We're on our way to a gig in Oneonta. We're supposed to play a show there tomorrow – I guess, really, today.. I sure didn't know we would end up here or that I would see you."

"A gig, huh?" Emma felt herself struggling to figure out what music he played. She recalled that he was always talking about his music, and she knew he majored in music at college, but once he stopped coming around, Emma had lost track of what he did.

"I didn't realize you played professionally," she added as she tried to focus on the computer screen in front of her.

"Yeah, we've been a band for a while now. Diagnosis?"

Emma stared blankly at Noah, even though she knew he expected her to recognize the band name.

"I... I don't really follow contemporary music much," Emma admitted. "Sorry."

"I don't know if you could say we're contemporary anymore," Noah said. Emma noticed he looked down at his shoes when he spoke about it, almost as if he were embarrassed. "We had a few hit songs, but that was years ago. So it doesn't really matter, I guess."

"Mom and Dad mostly listen to different stuff—classical, jazz, musicals, all that stuff. I'm… I'm sure you remember some of that," Emma said, feeling a blush rise to her cheeks.

"I do." Noah laughed. "Your dad would always try to have conversations with me about Bill Evans and Oscar Peterson and if I liked particular albums. Of course, Paul would always—"

Emma noticed a wince cross Noah's face as he mentioned Paul's name. She had become accustomed to the reaction any time anyone uttered his name over the last five years.

"Yeah, Paul was always embarrassed by Mom and Dad's musical tastes," Emma added, trying to turn the conversation around.

"How's he doing?" Noah said before catching himself. "Your Dad, I mean."

"Right." Emma straightened herself as she stood, trying not to choke up. "Dad's good. The same as ever. He works hard at the store every day, no matter what. I'm sure he'll insist on opening in the morning even if we have two feet on the ground. He never wants anyone to not be able to get something, you know. Of course, it gets busy, but he handles it all pretty well."

"Your mom doesn't work at the store anymore?"

Now it was Emma's turn to wince. She took a deep breath and looked into Noah's face.

"No, she stopped a couple of years ago. Turns out she has some heart issues. Genetic stuff she was born with and never knew about."

"Oh, I'm sorry, I didn't know," Noah spoke with concern.

You would have known if you had bothered to come, Emma thought.

"It's okay," Emma recovered. "We keep a close eye on her at home between me, Dad, and Hayley."

Noah chuckled.

"Hayley." He laughed. "She was always running around like a tornado, trying to put on skits when I came over. How is she?"

"She's a senior in high school now. Head cheerleader, probably the prom queen, that whole deal."

"Geez, a senior," Noah said with shock. "I can't believe it. Time went so fast."

"It sure did," Emma replied, focusing more on Noah's face now. Even though his eyes shone, they looked tired and worn. The brown beard he carried looked a little unkempt, his shoulders slumped. His smile, though, when it did peek out, still touched her.

"I can't believe it's really you." Noah smiled. "You're all grown up now."

"It does happen, you know," Emma said, unsure if she should feel flattered or offended.

"I know... I mean, of course, you would," Noah stammered. "It's just... it's nice to see you—a familiar face."

An awkward silence hung in there for far too long before Emma spoke up again.

"You probably want to get up to your room and rest. If you need anything, I'm down here until seven, when the day crew shows up. You can just press the phone button for the front desk."

Emma watched as Noah worked to stifle a yawn before he nodded yet again.

Emma's eyes followed Noah as he took several steps toward the elevator before he stopped and turned back toward her.

"Are you working tomorrow... I mean today, I guess?" Noah asked.

"I don't come on until eleven p.m.," Emma replied.

"So I might not get to see you before we head out then," Noah lamented.

"If the snow has stopped and the Thruway is cleared, no, you probably won't."

"I guess we'll see what the rest of the day brings us," Noah added. "Thanks, Twig."

Noah turned the corner, and Emma heard the elevator doors open and shut quickly.

"You're welcome. I guess," she answered.

****

Noah walked along the familiar streets of Emerald Lake, shuffling through the snow, viewing businesses and homes he had not seen in years. In minutes, he found himself standing before the Birch home, staring at the windows. Through the open window of the living room, the Christmas tree glistened brightly, even with the dull gray skies overhead. Noah watched from the sidewalk and caught a glimpse of Emma and her mother, Alice, walking from one side of the tree to the other. The smiles visible on their faces warmed Noah as snow fell around him. He noticed Emma turn toward the window and lock eyes with him, and her smile broadened. Her radiant image struck Noah in a manner he never expected, and when she waved to him to come to the house, he slowly made his way to the driveway that led to the path to the front door.

The snow seemed deeper as Noah slogged through, with drifts reaching nearly to his waist. He could barely make his way through it all as winds kicked up and brought down the snow harder. Noah inched forward, snow up to his chest now before he was stuck. He tried to yell out for help, but the howling wind drowned him out as the snow fell with greater intensity. Finally, the drift piled around him, and Noah no longer could see the house through the torrent around him. A gloved hand reached its way toward his body, but Noah's hands were numb from the cold and covered, so he could not reach out for help. As he struggled to free his hands, a buzzing sound began to circle his head. He glanced up through the snowfall and saw bees circling his head.

"What the fuck?" Noah exclaimed. "How are bees—"

Noah was cut off as the swarm thickened around him and approached with ferocity.

The angry buzzing increased as Noah screamed, bees flying toward his open mouth before he bolted upright in his bed, panting. Noah turned toward the buzzing he heard, seeing his cell phone vibrating on the nightstand next to his bed.

He breathed deeply several times before he reached for the phone jumping on the nightstand. He glanced at the phone and saw it was nearly eleven in the morning and that Jerry called him multiple times, including at the moment.

Noah clicked the answer button and worked on clearing his throat.

"Shit, Noah, it's about time you answered," Jerry yelled into the phone. "Where the fuck are you guys? No one else has picked up either."

"We're in Emerald Lake at a hotel," Noah answered groggily.

Noah turned and put his feet on the floor, walking over to the dark curtains and pulling them open. The sky was filled with white, blinding Noah briefly. Snow covered the ground below with few, if any, signs of life out and about.

"Where is that?" Jerry asked.

"It's a couple of hours south of Oneonta. Based on the way things look here, I doubt we're making it to the show tonight. Where are you?"

"I'm in Oneonta," Jerry answered. "I guess I was closer than I thought. It doesn't really matter, though. You guys aren't here, the equipment isn't here, and the show's been canceled. Too much lousy weather hanging around."

A sense of unexpected relief washed over Noah before he mustered a reply.

"Where's the rig with our stuff?"

"Somewhere much farther down on the Thruway. They barely got past Albany before they slid off the road. There's damage to the truck and some of the gear. It's going to cost us for sure."

Noah snapped to attention when he heard about the damaged gear.

"Is my piano okay?"

"No one told me there was anything wrong with it, so I'm going to assume it's good. I'll double-check to make sure."

"Please," Noah replied urgently.

Noah had brought his grand piano with them on tour for the last several years. While he hated moving it around so much, it was cheaper than renting one at each venue and hoping what was there met his needs and sound. He knew his instrument was perfect and savored every moment he spent with it.

"So what do we do now?" Noah asked Jerry.

"Well, I guess you guys hang tight where you are until the storm lets up and you can travel again. Weather forecasts say it can linger for another day or two. Who knows how long it will take to get roads cleared and our stuff repaired, especially with the holidays so close. We didn't have any gigs lined up until after the New Year anyway. The Oneonta payday would have been nice before Christmas."

Noah gave a slight nod, knowing some of the guys may have been counting on it more than others, particularly Ray, even if he wasn't aware of it. Jerry had long ago taken control of Ray's finances after burning through the money the band's early successes generated. But, on the other hand, Noah attempted to be smart with his investments once he got over the early awe of seeing the royalty checks and concert revenues. He built a nice nest egg for himself to fall back on at any moment, and since he was the writer of most of the band's hits of the past, he had extra income that the others may not see.

"Noah? You still there?" Jerry spoke, cutting through the silence.

"Yeah, sorry, I was just spacing," Noah admitted. "Not enough sleep, I guess."

"Well, you'll have plenty of time to make up for that stuck in your little town for a bit. I don't imagine there's much going on there that is going to keep you guys entertained."

"Yeah, I don't think so either," Noah replied, even though he was already plotting out just what he was going to do with part of his day.

After hanging up with Jerry and scrolling through some of the messages on his phone, Noah pulled on the waffle long-sleeve Henley and a pair of jeans he had in his bag. A quick glance in the mirror showed the extra stubble he had let grow scruffily on his face before he slipped back into his boots and headed out of the room.

With no messages from the rest of his bandmates, Noah meandered down to the lobby, checking the area around the front desk. There were no signs of Emma anywhere before Noah remembered her shift ended hours ago. A cheery face appeared from around the corner and greeted him.

"Good morning," the young woman added perkily. "Can I help you with anything?"

"No, I don't think so," Noah said, stretching as he looked at the front windows to see the snow still rapidly falling. "How much is out there?"

"Oh, it must be closing in on two feet by now," the girl remarked, craning her neck to look out the window before she shuffled out from behind the front desk. "Forecasters think we could get at least another six inches before it stops tonight."

"Wow," Noah answered, in awe of the snowfall amount he hadn't seen since his college days.

"It's been a while since you've been back this way, huh?" the girl asked sheepishly.

"Yeah. How did you know that?"

"I hope you don't think it's weird, but I am a massive fan of Diagnosis. I love your music."

Noah glanced at the woman, who looked to be no more than twenty. Her cheeks were flush with the embarrassment and awe Noah rarely saw on anyone's face when they met him nowadays.

"You—you actually know who we are?" Noah said with surprise.

"Are you kidding?" she said with shock. "As soon as Emma—she was the night manager here when you arrived—as soon as she told me this morning that you guys were here, I've been waiting for one of you to come down. I'm sorry. I don't mean to be gushing like this, but it's so rare that we actually get anyone famous rolling through our town. Kevin Bacon was up here shooting a movie for a few days a while back, but it wasn't nearly as exciting as this. At least not for me. Again, I don't mean to be rambling on like this. I'm Grace."

Grace presented her hand shakily to Noah. She beamed at him as Noah reached his hand out to her.

"I'm—"

"Oh, I know who you are." She giggled. "Noah Healy. This is so amazing," she gushed as she gripped Noah's hand tightly, holding on to it for a few extra beats. "I wish I knew you guys were here before I came in. I would've brought some CDs with me. You wouldn't mind signing them, would you? No, of course, you wouldn't. You're the nice guy of the band, right? Darn, I wish I had them here."

Grace stomped her foot lightly on the tile floor, the noise echoing through the empty room.

"Well, it looks like we might be here for a couple of days, so maybe if you bring them by tomorrow, I'd be happy to."

"Oh, this is too much!" she squealed. "Do you... do you think we could take a picture—please?"

"Sure," Noah acquiesced. He had recently grown accustomed to taking fan pictures since the band often did VIP packages that Jerry insisted on. The super fans would pay extra to get photo ops with the band, or, when they played smaller venues, the band was coerced into selling T-shirts and signing CDs after the show to make some extra cash.

Grace had quickly whipped out her cell phone and was draping an arm around Noah's shoulder, smiling up into the camera before Noah even had a chance to react. She snapped off one picture and then another right after, where Grace turned her head and planted a kiss on Noah's cheek. Noah barely had time to react to either one.

"I'm so sorry, but I just couldn't resist."

Noah watched as Grace looked at the photos with glee.

"My mom is going to freak," Grace added. "She'll be so jealous about this."

The phone behind the front desk rang and Grace scurried back to her post. Noah blankly stared out the front window, understanding that the band had become the one mothers and fathers listened to now. It was crushing enough when he first heard "My Temptation," one of the early hits he had written, turn up on an adult easy listening station.

Noah heard Grace clicking away on the computer at the front desk before he turned around.

"Grace, is the Birch Tree still right down the street?"

"Yep, right where it's always been," she said without missing a beat. "How do you know about the store? Oh, right, you used to be around here! I forgot you went to college up this way and knew the Birch family."

"How do you know that?" Noah asked with surprise.

"I told you I'm a fan," Grace said proudly. "Besides, my mom talked about you guys all the time. She must have said a hundred times that you hung around here before the band hit big. You were a friend of Paul Birch, right?"

Noah winced at the sting of the question before answering.

"Yeah. We were roommates in Oneonta."

"Right." Grace nodded. "Anyway, the store is down the street. The sidewalks were clear this morning when I came in, so you should be good to walk down. I don't know if you'll be warm enough in that coat, though."

Noah glanced down at his well-worn black leather jacket, taking in the cracks and faded spots.

"I'll be okay. Thanks for your help."

"You bet!" she said excitedly. "If you need anything—anything at all—just let me know. Do you think the other members will be down soon? I'd be glad to run out and grab them some lunch or something. I know Ray is very particular about what he eats for his meals. The diner makes some perfect salad, so I'm sure they can do it to his specifications—no cherry tomatoes, extra cucumber, only green olives, extra zesty Italian dressing, right?"

"I don't know. That sounds right," Noah replied. "I think you know more about his likes than I do. They'll probably be down soon enough. I'll see you later."

Noah walked out to the sidewalk and was greeted with a faceful of blowing snow and wind. He trudged up the sidewalk, taking care to step in the shoveled spots he could find to avoid slipping. He skidded in a couple of places where stores had not opened for the day. He eased up a bit as he passed the diner, noticing the fogged-over window. Noah peered in as he went by, spying a couple of people perched at the counter, hunched over steaming bowls of late breakfast or early lunch.

Noah hustled along, catching a glimpse of the Hidden Jewel Pub. He recalled the few times he and Paul had tried to sneak in when they were underage, and the one time they made it in when Paul's high school friend, working there as a waitress, let them in the back door so they could score a couple of drinks while listening to a jazz trio. Paul was more caught up in the free alcohol and flirting with the waitress, while Noah was enthralled with the skills of the piano player.

When he reached the front of the Birch Tree, Noah hesitated. Pellets of snow and sleet bounced off his leather jacket as he faced the front door, adorned with Christmas decorations. Noah considered turning back to the hotel but figured Emma likely mentioned to her family that she saw him in town. No matter how uncomfortable it might be for him, he felt an obligation to at least say hello.

Noah pulled open the door, the wind causing it to fly open wider than he had expected before he struggled to get it closed. The familiar jingle of the bells on the door loudly pealed out across the store. Noah glanced up but saw no one in sight. As the ringing died down, he could hear Burl Ives singing

"Holly Jolly Christmas" before a voice piped loudly from beyond.

"Be out in a second."

The friendly voice of Clay Birch was unmistakable to Noah, and he refrained from replying, looking around the store at the vast array of items that were always for sale there. The shop always looked to be the epitome of the small-town general store, offering a little of everything to accommodate the needs of locals and tourists alike.

Noah busied himself, looking over the scattered Hallmark ornaments that remained to be picked over by last-minute shoppers before Clay appeared from the back.

"Sorry about that," Clay offered. "I'm just trying to move some bags of sand and rock salt out in case anyone needs them. If you're looking for Christmas ornaments, it's slim pickings with the Hallmark stuff. But I've got some made locally by Edna Turnbull that are gorgeous if you'd like. They make a great gift."

Noah slowly turned to face Clay and gave a crooked smile.

"Hi, Mr. Birch," Noah announced.

Noah saw Clay stare back at him before the recognition hit. Surprise quickly turned to a smile, and Clay offered his right hand.

"Noah? By God, what are you doing here?"

"We were passing through the area, and the snowstorm kind of derailed us, and we ended up here. I'm staying down at the hotel. I'm surprised Emma didn't say something to you. I saw her last night—well, this morning—when we checked in."

Clay chuckled and smiled widely as he vigorously shook Noah's hand before moving in to give Noah a hug.

"Emma and I usually don't cross paths in the morning. I leave to open up here before she gets off her shift at the hotel. I can't believe you're here. How long has it been?"

Noah knew precisely how long it had been but played it down, shrugging his shoulders.

"Ten years, maybe more."

"Way too long, whatever it has been," Clay remarked.

The two men let an awkward silence pass between them as Burl Ives transitioned to "Rudolph the Red-Nosed Reindeer."

"So, how's the rock star life treating you? It's not too often we get a bona fide star traveling through the area. We did have—"

"Kevin Bacon?" Noah interjected.

"Yeah, how did you know?" Clay asked.

"Grace at the hotel told me."

"Ahh, Grace." Clay laughed. "Sweet girl, but she's a little too caught up in stuff like that if you ask me. Anyway... you're a music star now."

"I'd hardly say that, Mr. Birch," Noah answered humbly.

"Noah, you don't have to call me Mr. Birch. You're not a kid anymore. But you always did have the best manners of any of Paul's friends. Call me Clay."

Noah nodded.

"How long are you in town for?"

"I'm not sure. The show we had in Oneonta got canceled, and we're having trouble with our equipment trailer, so we might be here for a few days until the roads clear up and everything is fixed."

"Well, then you have to come for dinner—tonight, at least. Alice will be so thrilled to see you. It will be a great surprise for her."

"Oh, no, I couldn't," Noah said rapidly. "I might have stuff to do—"

"Don't be silly," Clay retorted. "I love the diner as much as the next guy, but you can't eat every meal from there. You probably haven't had a home-cooked meal in forever, am I right?"

Noah's version of a home-cooked meal when the band wasn't on the road usually consisted of whatever premade food he could get from the local supermarket or deli.

"Really, I don't want to put you out or anything. It's not a big deal."

"Noah, it is a big deal for me," Clay said as he stepped closer to Noah. "You were always like family to us. You know that. I won't take no for an answer."

"Fair enough," Noah caved.

"Great," Clay answered, clapping his hands together loudly. "I close up the shop at seven tonight. Come by, and I'll drive you over to the house. You'll never make it all the way without freezing in that coat of yours. Now, not to be rude, but I have to lug that rock salt out here. I know Erik Pederson will be in here to pick up bags before he goes out clearing driveways tonight."

Clay turned to go toward the back before Noah spoke up.

"Do—do you need a hand?" Noah asked. "I mean, I'm not doing anything. I'd be happy to help you out."

"Are you sure? I don't want you damaging your piano fingers moving bags. I know how delicate you musicians can be," Clay said with a wink.

Noah laughed before following Clay into the back room, feeling relief.

5

As was typical for Emma, she slept until three in the afternoon before getting up for the day. She had made sure her mother had everything she might need after getting home. Theoretically, Hayley was home on Christmas break to take care of anything her mother might need, and with the storm, it was unlikely any of them were going anywhere.

Emma ventured downstairs, cell phone in hand, wearing an oversized sweater and black leggings, her red hair tied back in a ponytail. The Christmas tree twinkled as she spied her mother's chair empty. When she saw no one in the kitchen, a moment of panic crossed her mind. She paced down to her parents' bedroom, giving a gentle knock before pushing the door open. She saw her mother sleeping peacefully, enjoying an afternoon nap. Emma sighed, relieved, before shutting the door and moving back to the kitchen.

Emma pried open the fridge to see what she had around to cook for dinner tonight. Meals usually fell to her, especially since her mother became ill. Emma thoroughly enjoyed the moments she got to cook and meal plan. She set about taking an array of vegetables out of the fridge, along with some stew beef, deciding it was the perfect day for a meal of beef stew and some homemade biscuits. She planted her phone in the docking station on the kitchen counter and put on her favorite Christmas playlist before she started in on peeling and chopping.

Before Emma knew it, the meat was cooking in the Dutch oven she set on the stovetop. First, she removed the beef and added the vegetables, allowing the aroma of onions to permeate the air before sprinkling some flour on top of the nicely browning vegetables. Next, Emma pulled a couple of the quarts of homemade beef stock she had on hand and poured them into the pot, eliciting steam and sizzle before adding the meat back in, along with some spices. The bubbling stew was then left to its own devices to cook for hours while she plucked out her phone and a gingerbread cookie before climbing onto the couch to gaze mindlessly at social media.

Emma didn't take long to come across a post her coworker Grace had put up on Facebook. There Grace was, grinning wildly, with an arm wrapped around Noah Healy. The following picture showed Grace kissing his cheek while Noah had his eyes shut. Grace went on to brag about the encounter and about how they had celebrities staying at the hotel.

Emma scrolled past the post to see what else was going on, checking out pictures of dogs romping in the snow or questions about whether the diner was open or not before she went back to the image. She studied it, looking at the non-smile Noah flashed.

She felt a distant sadness in the way he appeared and wished she had more time to get to talk with him.

She closed her social media and decided to do some searching regarding Diagnosis online. She quickly found the band's homepage, reading the hyped-up bio on the front pages and talking about the last release they had, which looked to be three years ago. There were still photos of Noah and the other members, but all the pictures appeared to be several years old and showed them smiling or mugging for the camera. Next, Emma looked into the band's tour schedule and saw their recent shows all seemed to be small venues.

Jumping back to her search engine, Emma gazed at some reviews for the band's last album, titled "Bend Her Backward." Unfortunately, critics were less than kind about the release, and even diehard fans seemed to remark on forums that the band was "clearly on its last legs."

Emma went to her streaming service and selected the album to see what it was like. She tried to make it through several songs but found nothing that sounded like she had hoped. The music was loud, frenetic, and seemingly pieced together. She could not imagine the voice coming out of the man who was the band's lead singer that she had come across the previous night.

Instead of giving up completely, she went back through the band's catalog of albums, going to their first release, simply called "Diagnosis." It was there that Emma was surprised to hear music far different from what the band released over the last few years. The songs were more melodic, had meaning and depth to them, and pulled her in. Noah could easily be heard playing his heart out on the piano, and there were even a couple of tunes that stood out to her because the piano was at the forefront of the music.

After putting the music aside and just watching the snowfall out the window for a while, Emma went about straightening up the living room and dining room before she heard the familiar movement of her mother's walker coming down the hall.

"Need help, Mom?" Emma shouted as she folded one of the Christmas throws and placed it over the back of the couch.

"I'm fine, Emma," her mother yelled back, a tinge of annoyance in her voice. "You don't have to check on me constantly, you know," her mother added as she appeared in the doorway to the living room.

"I wasn't checking on you," Emma answered, looking up.

"You were when you opened the bedroom door earlier." Her mother moved the walker over in front of her recliner before easing herself down into the seat.

"How do you know that? You were sound asleep."

"I'm never sound asleep." Her mother smirked. "I hear a lot more going on than you think. The stew smells wonderful, by the way."

Emma glanced at her phone and saw it was nearly six.

"Do you need anything?" she asked. "I'm going in to make biscuits."

"Go, go." Her mother waved.

Emma pulled out her stainless steel mixing bowl and grabbed her ingredients, including the buttermilk, so she could mix everything. She found herself putting music on this time, but she was listening to Diagnosis instead of Christmas. Hayley wandered into the kitchen as Emma cut the biscuit rounds and placed them on a baking sheet. Her sister stopped cold and stared at her.

"What?" Emma asked as she blew a strand of hair off her forehead.

"What are you listening to?" Hayley questioned.

"Music," Emma added casually and went back to cutting biscuits.

"No kidding," Hayley answered sarcastically. "It's not Christmas music. That's all you've been listening to since Thanksgiving dinner. You don't even like rock music."

Hayley walked closer to the counter and glanced at Emma's phone to see what was playing.

"Diagnosis? Since when do you even know who they are?"

"I thought I would try something new," Emma said defensively. "What's the difference?"

"They're relics, is all," Hayley scoffed. "No one listens to them anymore."

"I don't know about that. They have some good songs."

"Whatever," Hayley said with an eye roll, raising her hand at her sister.

"Can you just set the table, please?" Emma asked as Hayley left the kitchen.

"Can't you do it?" Hayley whined. "I've got a call with Madison."

"Fine," Emma mumbled under her breath.

Emma grabbed four bowls from the cabinet and dashed to the dining room, laying out the place settings with small plates for the biscuits and getting cutlery before returning to the kitchen to put the biscuits in the oven.

It was just a bit after seven when Emma heard the familiar rumble of her father's truck settling into his usual spot in the driveway.

"Your father's home," her mother shouted from the living room.

"I hear him," Emma replied before grabbing the pot of stew off the stove. Her hands, covered in snowman oven mitts, gripped the handles and gingerly carried the stew to the dining room before placing it down on the matching snowman trivet. Emma heard the front door open and close and some brief commotion as she reached into the oven to pull out the biscuits. The golden brown color was perfect, and Emma placed the soft pillows of dough into the breadbasket before making her way to the dining room.

"Dinner's ready!" Emma yelled as she made sure the pile of biscuits looked perfect as her family walked into the dining room.

"Can you set another place?" Emma heard her father ask before she looked up.

"Sure—" Emma began as she turned her eyes toward her father and spotted Noah standing next to him.

Words stuck in Emma's throat as she gazed at Noah. She noticed a slight smile sneak across his lips.

"Hi again," Noah stated.

"Hi," Emma croaked out. "Let me get a setting for you."

Emma dashed off into the kitchen, grabbing an extra bowl and pulling open the cutlery drawer to get a knife, spoon, and fork. She immediately dropped the knife, letting it clang onto the floor before bending over to pick it up. As she rushed back up, she smacked the back of her head on the still-open drawer.

"Shit!" she yelled as she dropped the cutlery once again, this time adding the bowl to the pile on the linoleum.

"Emma Louise!" her mother shouted from the dining room. "Language, please!"

Clay walked into the kitchen while still talking to Noah.

"Can I get you a beer, Noah?" Clay asked as he came in and saw Emma squatting on the floor, rubbing the back of her head.

"You okay?" Clay asked, helping Emma to her feet.

"Peachy," she mumbled as she tossed the dropped items into the sink and grabbed others. "Why didn't you say you were bringing a guest home?"

"What guest?" Clay asked, pulling two bottles of beer out. "It's Noah. He's not a guest. He's family."

"No offense, Dad, but he hasn't been around in ten years. That's not really family. A little notice would have been nice. I would have cooked more and made some dessert, and I certainly wouldn't be walking around looking like this," she said with a tug on her baggy sweater.

"Stop, you look fine," Clay said, brushing Emma off. "I'm sure he's seen you in worse when you were a kid."

"That's not helping any, Dad," Emma replied. She took a moment to tie her ponytail more neatly before going back into the dining room.

"Here you go," Emma said, placing everything in front of Noah, who was now seated directly across from her at the table.

"Sorry to cause you trouble," Noah offered.

"No trouble at all." Emma smiled, sitting and taking a deep breath. Clay reentered the dining room and placed one of the beer bottles in front of Noah.

"Where's Hayley?" Clay asked, looking to his left at the empty seat at the table.

"Probably up in her room gossiping," Emma said as she ladled some stew into her mother's bowl.

"Can you get her?" Alice remarked.

Clay took two steps toward the stairs and shouted, "Hayley, hustle up! Dinner!"

"I could have done that," Alice bemoaned.

"No, you couldn't have," Clay replied. "I have a much louder voice than you. She would never hear you." Clay smiled as he blew Alice a kiss.

Hayley bounced down the steps, staring at her phone, and sat at her seat at the table. When she looked up, she saw Noah sitting there at the table.

"Whoa," Hayley said as she looked at Noah.

"Hayley, do you remember Noah?" Alice said as she passed the plate of biscuits to Noah.

"Vaguely," she answered in passing.

"You were pretty little the last time I saw you," Noah admitted.

"I guess so." Hayley shrugged. "You're Paul's friend, the one who plays the piano, right?"

Noah nodded as he pried open a biscuit, sending steam up from the table.

"He doesn't just play," Clay said as he filled his spoon with stew. "He's in a famous rock band."

"I wouldn't say that," Noah answered humbly.

"What band?" Hayley asked.

"Diagnosis," Noah replied. "You've probably never heard of us."

Hayley shot a look over at Emma and smiled.

"Sure, I've heard of you guys." Hayley grinned. "Old-school rock. It's funny because Emma and I—"

Emma stretched her right foot over and stepped on Hayley's left foot, eliciting a "Hey!" from her sister.

"Hayley, can you help me in the kitchen?" Emma said, standing up. "I forgot the salt and pepper."

"You know where they are," Hayley said.

"Come help me anyway," Emma insisted, pulling her sister from her chair and tugging her toward the kitchen.

"What the hell, Em?" Hayley said, grabbing the salt and pepper shakers off the counter. "I think you can handle carrying them."

"You don't need to talk about me listening to their music," Emma asked as she grabbed some more paper napkins from the cabinet.

"You knew he was in town, didn't you?" Hayley smirked.

"They came into the hotel late last night, so yes," Emma admitted. "It's no big deal."

"Doesn't seem that way to me. You had a crush on Noah when we were younger, didn't you?"

"That was a long time ago," Emma stated firmly. "I was just a kid."

"Right, and then, all of a sudden, you're listening to his music—music you don't even know or like. You're still crushing on him!"

"No, no, I'm not," Emma insisted, trying to hush her sister. "Let's just drop it, okay?"

"Fine," Hayley agreed. "I won't say anything. But you owe me."

"Owe you for what?"

"For not commenting on how you're going to make eyes at Noah while he's here."

"That won't happen."

Emma straightened her back and marched into the dining room, bringing extra napkins while Hayley carried the salt and pepper.

"What took you two so long?" Clay asked, picking up the pepper and putting a dose on his stew.

"Just sister talk," Emma said before Hayley had a chance to make a remark. "Eat up."

"The stew is great," Noah said between spoonfuls. He looked toward Alice as he made the remark.

"It's all Emma," Alice said proudly. "She's such a good cook. Oh, and her baking. Her baking is out of this world. Of course, you'll have to try her muffins."

Hayley coughed and suppressed a laugh.

"Yeah, Noah. I'm sure Emma would be happy to have you try her muffin."

The heat rose to Emma's face as she blushed and shot daggers at her sister.

"Sure," Noah answered, seemingly oblivious to the remark.

Hayley could barely contain herself now, and Emma reached her right hand across to Hayley's under the table and grabbed it to get her attention. Emma mouthed "No" as harshly and silently as she could.

The rest of the meal passed with quiet conversation. Alice and Clay peppered Noah with questions about his travels and career. Emma found herself caught up in his stories as well as he spoke of the band's days of international travel and arena concerts.

Everyone sat around the table with empty bowls and crumbs on their plates, with just two biscuits remaining on the plate.

Emma had just picked up the remains of her biscuit when Hayley spoke.

"So you must have a lot of women throwing themselves at you all the time, Noah, being a rock star and all."

Emma coughed on what she was eating and her mother chimed in.

"Hayley, that's not really an appropriate question to ask," Alice scolded. "Noah, I'm sorry."

"It's okay." Noah chuckled, wiping his face with his napkin. "The groupie days are long over. I don't really get any of that anymore."

"So you used to, though, huh?" Hayley asked. "Girls showing up in your hotel room kind of thing, tossing their panties at you?"

"Hayley!" Alice said sternly.

"I'm just curious, is all," Hayley defended. "You hear about this stuff. I was just wondering if it was true."

"I think a lot of that is pretty exaggerated," Noah told her.

"You're saying if some pretty woman showed up at your hotel tonight, you would turn her away?"

Hayley rested her chin in the palms of her hands, glanced at Emma, and awaited Noah's answer.

"I don't think I have to worry about that." Noah laughed.

"I wouldn't be too sure," Hayley added. Emma shot up from the table.

"I'll clear the table and make coffee," she spouted. "Hayley, you help," Emma said through gritted teeth as she shoved a couple of stacked bowls into her sister's hands.

Emma quickly gathered up the dishes and pushed her sister toward the kitchen. After moving Hayley along toward the sink, Emma reached the dishwasher and pulled the door open. She also turned on the faucet to help drown out what she wanted to say.

"You're an ass." Emma scowled.

"Oh stop, I'm just teasing you," Hayley said as she opened the cabinet to grab some containers to store the leftovers in. "How often do I get a chance to do this? You never fawn over a guy."

"I'm not fawning over anyone!"

Emma crammed the dishes into the dishwasher roughly before kicking the door closed. Then, she marched over to the coffeemaker and began to set it up. She grabbed the container of gingerbread cookies and began to put some on a platter, alongside a couple of the blueberry muffins she had made.

"Ooh, getting your goodies out for Noah?" Hayley said seductively.

"Oh my God, I'm going to strangle you!" Emma blurted out, tossing a muffin at her sister. Hayley dodged to her left, and the muffin whizzed past her, striking their father, who was entering the kitchen.

"Interesting way to bring dessert out," Clay said as he plucked the muffin off the floor. "What is up with you two tonight?"

"Emma can't take it as well as she can dish it out, is all." Hayley smirked.

"What is that supposed to mean?" Clay asked.

"Nothing, Dad," Emma interrupted. "Can you bring the coffee mugs out? I'll get the rest."

"Sure," Clay answered, confusion in his voice.

"Hayley, please," Emma begged. "No more. Let's just get through this night. I have to leave for work in an hour or so, and then this will all be over."

"I don't know. Dad made it sound like Noah was going to be around for a few days. Between the weather and whatever is wrong with their truck, you might have him in your face—but I don't think you'll mind."

"Grrrr!" Emma growled before she grabbed the plate of desserts and marched back to the dining room.

6

Gratefulness reigned supreme for Emma once dinner was completed. She thanked the heavens when Hayley's cell phone buzzed and her sister dashed upstairs to chat with her friends, leaving Emma alone with her parents and Noah. Once dinner was all cleaned up, Emma had to pry herself away so she could shower and change for work.

She did all she could to put everything out of her head and think about the tasks she had to take care of tonight, trying not to consider Noah at all. But as soon as she got out of the shower and walked toward her room upstairs, clad in her robe, she could hear that Noah remained in the house, laughing and chatting with her folks.

Emma donned her standard black dress pants but added some Christmas flair by wearing a red button-down blouse and candy cane earrings before putting her hair up in a bun. She packed her bag with her supplies for work and padded down the steps to see Noah sitting on the sofa, the fireplace roaring and the Christmas tree in all its glory.

Clay looked up and caught a glimpse of his daughter and smiled.

"Time to leave for work already?" he asked.

"Yeah, Bernadette wanted me to get in earlier because Marianne hasn't been able to get in." Emma shrugged.

"Do you want me to drive you?"

"Come on, Dad, you know I don't. But thanks for asking. Besides, it looks like the snow has finally stopped. I'm fine to walk."

Emma saw Noah rise from the couch.

"I should probably get going as well," Noah indicated. "I'm sure the guys are looking for me."

Emma watched as Noah walked over and bent down and gave her mother a kiss on the cheek.

"Thanks for having me over," Noah told her.

"Oh, it was so good to see you, Noah," Alice beamed. "Please make sure you stop in again before you leave town."

"I will, I promise."

Clay walked over to the coat closet by the front door and grabbed Noah's leather jacket.

"You're going to freeze to death in this thing," Clay said as he looked over the ragged jacket. It's pretty cold out now. Let me drive you."

"No, it's not necessary," Noah insisted.

"Clay, get him a proper jacket," Alice pressed. Clay went back into the closet and pulled out a red flannel fleece-lined jacket. Emma watched as he moved toward Noah and began to choke up.

"Here," Clay said, presenting the jacket to Noah. "This will keep you plenty warm."

Emma saw the recognition in Noah's eyes.

"I can't take Paul's jacket," Noah resisted. "Mine is fine, really."

"Noah, please, take it," Alice remarked from her seat. "If anyone should wear it, it's you."

"Mom, don't force him," Emma said, her voice cracking.

"It's fine, really," Clay told him, pushing the jacket into Noah's hands. "It seems right."

Noah took the jacket and reluctantly donned it, slowly zipping it up.

"I promise, I'll bring it back before I leave town," Noah said as he moved toward the door.

"That's perfect." Clay smiled. "Have a good night, Noah. Honey, have a good night," Clay told Emma, giving her a hug.

"Call me when you get to work!" Alice shouted as Emma went out the front door that was held open by Noah.

Emma walked along the pathway in front of Noah, reaching the sidewalk before him. Noah pushed forward once they came to the concrete, matching Emma's stride, and was next to her.

"Dinner was fantastic," Noah said. "I had no idea you were such a good cook."

"Thanks. I love to cook and bake. And, of course, you had no idea what I could do. The last time you saw me, I was what, fourteen?"

"True," Noah lamented. "I'm... I'm sorry about that."

"About what?" Emma said casually. "You had your career getting off the ground and going. You didn't have any reason to come back here."

"That's not entirely true. I should have... I should have come back for Paul's funeral. So there's no excuse for not doing that. Or coming to see him before he died."

"He wasn't really here much after you guys left school," Emma said, working to control her emotions. "Once he left and joined the Army, he was in training and then assigned all over the place before he went to Afghanistan. So it would have been tough for you to catch him when he was here on leave."

"I just want you to know that I've never felt right about it," Noah told her.

The two had crossed the street and approached the Birch Tree storefront. Emma paused, as usual, at the front windows to look at the displays.

"Your dad does a great job with the windows for Christmas," Noah stated.

"He does"—Emma nodded—"but I do most of the design and setup."

"Really?" Noah said with surprise. "I had no idea. How long have you done that?"

"Since I was about twelve." Emma laughed.

"Well, it was always decorated by the time Paul and I came back for the break. I guess I just never saw you doing any of it. I probably didn't notice you doing a lot of things."

"Story of my life." Emma sighed as they walked on.

"No, I didn't mean it like that," Noah added as he tried to recover. Emma smiled to herself, knowing she had flustered him. "I was always doing stuff with Paul, and you were younger, you know? You were always just the little sister. I probably should have been nicer to you, is all."

"Honestly, Noah, out of all of Paul's friends, you were the nicest one to me. Most of them just ignored me completely or had snide remarks about how skinny, tall, or flat-chested I was. You were at least friendly—and kind."

The two moved along the sidewalk until they were just outside the Hidden Jewel Pub.

"Do you really have to get to the hotel this early and start work?" Noah asked.

Emma glanced at her watch and saw it was only 9:45.

"I have a little time, I guess."

"Do you want to go in and have a drink?" Noah remarked.

"Yeah?"

"Why? Is that a problem? I don't want to get you in trouble if you can't have a drink before work."

"No, it's not that," Emma replied. "I don't go here very often. I don't think anyone has ever asked me to go for a drink with them at the pub, is all."

"Maybe it's a night of firsts." Noah smiled, holding the door open for Emma.

Emma walked into the dark pub and made her way toward the bar to grab a seat. The black and oak of the bar made the room seem cave-like as she sat on one of the leather stools. Noah walked up beside her and sat down, unzipping the flannel jacket. Emma removed her scarf and opened her coat so that her red satin blouse shimmered a bit in the overhead lighting.

Only one other patron sat at the end of the bar, while two couples occupied tables in front of the stage where spotlights pointed. The bartender, an older gentleman with snow-white hair and a beard to match, came down and stood in front of Emma and Noah. Emma smiled when she saw the bartender.

"Hi, Nick." Emma grinned.

"Emma? Wow, you're a sight for sore eyes. I haven't seen you in here in months. What's the occasion?"

"An old friend is in town and wanted to see the place. Noah Healy, this is Nick Klaus. He owns the pub," Emma commented.

Nick held his hand out to Noah, but Emma noticed Noah just staring at the man.

"Don't take this the wrong way," Noah began, "but your name is really Nick... Nick Klaus? And you have a white beard and hair, and well... you're a little—"

"Portly?" Nick chuckled.

"Yeah, portly," Noah added.

"It's okay. I get it all the time from outsiders." Nick laughed. "Santa has to do something in his downtime, right? So why not own a pub?"

"Now, I don't know if you're pulling my leg or not," Noah said seriously.

"Good!" Nick added a big belly laugh for emphasis. "What can I get you?"

"Do you have any scotch?" Noah asked as Emma watched him crane his neck at the top shelf behind Nick.

"Sure do," Nick said. "I don't get much of a call for the good stuff with the usual riffraff in here, but I've got it."

"Macallan, with a bit of ice?"

"You got it. How about you, Emma?"

"It's okay if you just want a soda or something," Noah told her. Emma squinted her eyes at him.

"I'm no lightweight, Mr. Rock and Roll," Emma challenged. "I'll have the same as him, Nick."

"Coming up," Nick said as he walked off to pour.

"You drink scotch?" Noah asked, bewildered.

"I'm not fourteen, Noah," Emma chimed in, taking off her coat. "I do a lot of things."

"Fair enough," Noah answered as Nick placed the drinks in front of them.
Noah lifted his glass and held it up to Emma.

"Cheers," Noah said.

"You mean to a night of firsts, don't you?" Emma smiled.

"That too," Noah told her before he clinked glasses with her.

Emma took the initial sip of scotch, something she had never had before, and felt the slow burn cross her tongue and ease down her throat before reaching her stomach. The warmth spread rapidly, and Emma worked not to cough so Noah would consider her a seasoned whisky drinker.

"You have a band tonight?" Emma remarked to Nick as he dried some glassware.

"We were supposed to," Nick stated. "Two of the guys are here, sitting at the table over there." Nick pointed to the far corner next to the stage. "The third guy is snowed in somewhere. They got mad when I said I was paying for a trio tonight, not just a bassist and drummer."

"Too bad," Emma said as she took another sip. She glanced at Noah and saw him take a long draw on his drink before he stood up and walked toward the men at the corner table.

"Noah, what are you—" Emma began, but Noah was already at the other table, talking to the men. Noah walked back toward the bar and looked at Nick.

"Will you pay them if I sit in and play a couple of songs with them?" Noah asked.

"It depends," Nick said skeptically. "Are you any good, or are you just messing with me because of the Santa Claus thing?"

"I can play." Noah smiled.

Emma saw Nick turn to her for affirmation.

"I've never seen him play in person, but I've heard he's good," Emma vouched.

"Two songs," Nick said, holding up two fingers. "If the songs are good, you get paid for the night along with them."

"I don't need it," Noah added. "Give them the whole amount, and it's a deal."

"Have at it, Music Man," Nick challenged, pointing to the stage.

Emma looked on as Noah sauntered up onto the stage, where the two young men had already taken their positions, one holding his upright bass while the other slid behind the drum kit.

Noah placed his hands above the piano's keys and did some test scales to see how it sounded. Then he nodded at the two other players and readied himself while the drummer counted them off.

Emma watched as Noah dove right in, playing the unfamiliar sound to Emma but clearly recognizable to both the other players and Nick. Noah closed his eyes as he played, letting the music guide him as he got swept into the rhythm he experienced. After a few minutes, the few patrons in the place, including Emma, were mesmerized by his performance.

"Why didn't you tell me your friend was a jazz pianist?" Nick said quietly to Emma. "He hoodwinked me."

"I knew he played piano," Emma confessed, "but I didn't know he could play jazz piano, honest."

"He's not just playing, Em," Nick said seriously. "He's in it."

The song seemed like it finished as fast as it had begun, with applause from the audience louder than Emma expected. She watched as Noah opened his eyes and smiled in her direction. He placed his hand over the microphone, covering it, so no one could hear what he was saying to the bass player and drummer. The other members nodded in agreement and waited for Noah to take the lead.

It only took a few notes from the piano for Emma to recognize the song and break out into a big smile. Then Noah began playing "Christmastime is Here," the Charlie Brown Christmas staple. The drummer gently brushed on the drums as the bassist strummed, and Noah played before he started to lightly sing the song. Emma's heart swelled as she closed her eyes to listen. Then, when the singing stopped and the music took over, she opened her eyes again to see Noah, light shining down on him, playing passionately before he finished the lyrics and brought the song to a close.

Noah stood up from the piano bench, shook hands with the bassist and drummer, and acknowledged the applause from the smattering of people present. Emma grinned at him as he sat back on his barstool and finished his scotch before Nick came over.

"Friend, if you want to keep playing, go right ahead," Nick said, pouring another scotch for Noah. "This one's on me. Money well spent."

Noah nodded as he picked up the glass and took another sip as Emma just stared at him.

"You're really good, aren't you?" she asked softly.

"Well, I've been playing for a long time," Noah answered.

"That's not what I mean," Emma said, becoming serious. "I mean, you're better than what you do now—what you've ever done—with rock music."

"I don't know about that." Noah laughed. "I like to think I'm pretty good at rock music. We did have hit records, you know, even if you never listened to them."

"I'll make a confession," Emma said as she finished her drink. "I listened to some of Diagnosis when I got home today. The new stuff and the old stuff."

"Ah, so that's what Hayley was getting at today."

"Yes, I'm sorry. I was embarrassed that I had never listened to it before or knew anything about it."

"So what did you think?" Noah asked matter-of-factly.

"Honestly?" Emma said reluctantly.

"Be truthful. I can take it. I've taken it for the last ten years or so," Noah admitted.

"Your new stuff—it's kind of disappointing. There's no feeling in the music. You can tell you guys are just going through the motions. And the lyrics to the songs! They're—"

"Absurd?" Noah said.

"Yes, but also kind of sexist and degrading at times. Why did you do that?"

"I didn't," Noah responded. "I didn't write any of those songs. Jerry, our manager, got them from some hit machine songwriter because I hadn't been able to come up with anything new. They're shit, but we had to record something. We had a contract and a deadline."

"Your early stuff, that first album was so much better," Emma told him. "You could tell your heart was in it, and you were really enjoying it."

"Yeah, that was when we were at our best," Noah admitted. "It was still new, and I could write better songs back then. Hell, I could just plain write songs then. The second album was good, too. But after that, I don't know, everything started to fall apart."

"How come?" Emma knew she was prying at this point, but her curiosity got the better of her.

"Oh, lots of reasons, I guess," Noah said evasively. "It's hard to pinpoint just one thing."

"What year was that at? The third album and all?"

Emma saw the hesitation on Noah's face.

"Twenty sixteen," he said as he drained the last of his drink.

"The year Paul died," Emma said softly.

"Among other things, yes," Noah said before he got up from his stool. "You must need to get to work," he added, abruptly changing the subject.

Noah reached into his wallet and pulled out two twenties and left them on the bar.

"You don't have to buy my drink," Emma insisted, going into her purse.

"Don't be ridiculous," Noah answered, holding up Emma's coat to help her put it on.

"Thanks, Nick," Emma said as they began to leave, waving to Nick as he poured a beer for someone at the bar.

"My pleasure," Nick shouted. "Seriously, Noah. If you ever want to come back and play, just ask. I'll find time to fit you in."

"I appreciate it. Thanks." Noah waved casually as he held the door open for Emma.

Transitioning back into the cold weather was something of a shock for Emma, even though she had spent most of her life doing just that. Something about being in the pub, being with Noah, watching him, made her feel warmer than usual. She couldn't wait to reach the hotel so she could take her coat off again and cool down some.

No sooner had she walked through the door, laughing with Noah beside her, when she was confronted by Bernadette.

"Emma? Where have you been? I needed you here," she shouted.

Emma nervously looked at her watch and saw it was still five to eleven.

"I'm not on the clock until eleven," she answered.

"I know, but with Marianne not here for the afternoon and evening, there's too much to do. You said you were going to come in early today to help out. I was counting on you," Bernadette barked.

Emma struggled to find an answer, but Noah stepped up.

"Bernadette, is it?" Noah asked as he glanced at the name tag. "I'm sorry, Bernadette. It's entirely my fault. See, I'm with the band that came in last night, and I was looking for something to do to kill some time since we can't go anywhere. Grace, the girl who was here this morning, was kind enough to let me know that Emma was a lifetime town resident and could help me get a meal and pick up a few things I needed. I kept her out so long, so you have my apologies. I'm sure we can make it up to you. I'm more than happy to talk to your office and tell them how accommodating your entire staff, especially you, have been to us so far."

Emma saw that Noah had disarmed Bernadette completely, turning everything around to make her and the hotel look better than ever.

"Well, thank you, Mr...." Bernadette struggled to recall the name.

"Healy. I'm Noah Healy," he said, introducing himself and shaking her hand. "I'm one of the founders of the band and the piano player. Can we take a picture maybe to send to your office or put on your social media?"

Before Bernadette even had a chance to react, Noah had put his arm around her and pointed to Emma to take a picture. Emma snapped off a few photos, all of which had Noah smiling widely while Bernadette stood with an uncomfortable confusion on her face.

"Perfect," Emma said. She quickly sent the photos to Bernadette via text so that the manager's phone could be heard dinging in the distance.

Completely disarmed, Bernadette stood befuddled for a second before going to the back office to check her phone.

"Thank you for that." Emma sighed to Noah. "She would have yelled at me relentlessly if you weren't here to do that."

"Not a problem." Noah smiled. "I'm glad your dad invited me to dinner. It was nice to see you—I mean, the family—again. I missed that."

Emma heard her left foot shuffling on the floor as she searched for something more to say.

"I should probably get to work."

"Oh, of course," Noah said. "I'm sure the guys have been looking for me all day anyway. Of course, I didn't expect to be hauling rock salt when I woke up this morning."

"I'm sorry if Dad kept you," Emma apologized. "He was just happy to see you and wanted to talk."

"It was okay. I liked spending time with your dad. He's always been one of my favorite people. The whole family is. I forgot how much I missed this."

"Good night, Noah." Emma smiled as she turned to go to the front desk. She scurried off to the front desk before looking back and seeing him still watching her. She kicked off her boots and slid into her flat shoes as he began to move toward the elevators. Noah's steps echoed on the floor before the footsteps ended, causing Emma to look up and see him standing right near the desk, startling her.

"Are you doing anything tomorrow?" he asked.

"Well, I get off work at seven in the morning," Emma explained. "I usually go home and sleep for a bit after I get Mom set up for the morning. With Hayley home for Christmas break, I get some extra rest. So no, I don't have anything planned, really. Last-minute Christmas stuff, I guess. It's only three days away."

"Okay," Noah began. "Since it looks like we're going to be here for a few more days at least, I thought maybe you might want to do something—together. We could get breakfast or lunch or whatever works for you. Unless you want to go home and sleep, of course. I get it if you do."

"No," Emma replied rapidly. "I mean, yes, I would love to do something. You can meet me at the house if you want at whatever time might be good for you."

"How about I just meet you here at seven when you get off work? I'd be glad to walk you home or get breakfast or whatever, and then we can spend the day together."

Stunned by Noah's offer, Emma stood unsure of what to say.

"Are you sure?" Emma asked.

"Yeah, why not?"

"It's just that, I don't know," Emma stuttered. "I figured you had stuff you needed to do with your friends or with work."

"Our show was canceled, and we have nothing until after the first of the year," Noah told her. "I have nothing but time on my hands right now. Besides, I've spent the last two months crammed on a bus with those guys, spending twenty-four seven together. We could use some time apart, trust me. So what do you say?"

Emma smiled at the offer.

"I say I'll see you at seven."

"Great," Noah beamed. "I hope you have a good night."

Noah walked off toward the elevators, and Emma heard the familiar ding of the arrival button.

"I already have," Emma whispered happily to herself.

7

Noah arrived back at his room only to find Edgar perched on the floor in front of the door. Edgar sat with his Air Pods in his ears, mindlessly drumming along with whatever he was listening to, his eyes closed. It wasn't until Noah tapped his bandmate with the tip of his boot that Edgar noticed him and stood up.

"Jesus, man, where have you been all day?" Edgar said as he rose from the floor. "I've called and texted a bunch of times."

Noah patted down the jacket and pants he wore, realizing he did not have his cell phone with him. He pulled the card key out of his front jeans pocket to open the door.

"I must have left my phone in here when I went out today. Sorry," Noah said as he entered the room.

"What's with the flannel jacket?" Edgar asked, following Noah inside.

"It's cold out. I needed something warmer," Noah answered defensively, taking care to remove the jacket and fold it nicely before placing it on the chair nearest the window. Then he went over to the nightstand and picked up his phone, seeing the myriad of texts and missed calls not just from Edgar but from Cecil, Jerry, and the other band members.

"I assume you heard the show was canceled," Edgar said as he sat down on the edge of Noah's bed.

"Yeah, I talked to Jerry this morning. But, unfortunately, he didn't have much good news to share about anything."

"It gets worse," Edgar said as he watched Noah plop down on the bed and stretch out.

"Now what?" Noah bemoaned.

"Jerry says the trailer is in bad shape. It's going to take them a while to fix it and cost a good chunk of change. Some of my drum kit got damaged, too, along with some of the amps and speakers. Insurance will cover some of it, but it's still a pain in the ass. And then there's Ray."

"What's up with Ray?" Noah sighed, rubbing his temples.

"The usual bullshit," Edgar added. "He wants his prima donna treatment no matter where we go, and in this hick town, there isn't much of that going on. He's had Cecil running and on the phone all day to track down things he wants to eat, clothes he needs, stuff he has to have for his room—you name it."

"It's not really a hick town," Noah said quietly. "It's a pretty nice place if you give it a chance."

"Is that what you were doing all day? Giving it a chance?"

"Look, I never told you guys any of this because you joined the band after Jack and I got things started at Oneonta, but I spent time here when I was younger. One of my best friends and my college roommate was from here, so I visited Emerald Lake a few times before leaving school. I still know a few people here."

"Okay, cool," Edgar replied, nodding. "So you spent the day catching up with an old buddy. Nothing wrong with that."

"Nah... he's—he's not around anymore," Noah answered, looking over at the flannel jacket. "I talked to his family. His parents are still here, along with his sisters. I had dinner and spent the day with them."

"Sisters, huh? Are they cute?"

"One of them is barely eighteen," Noah chided. "The other—well, the other is the woman who was at the front desk last night."

"The tall chick?" Edgar asked. "She was nice. Very friendly and helpful to us and pretty too. How well do you know her?"

"Not very well," Noah admitted. "Until last night, I hadn't seen her since she was fourteen. Twig was always a nice girl, kind of shy, but friendly, you know?"

"Her name is Twig?"

Noah laughed out loud when he heard it.

"No, no." He chuckled. "Her real name is Emma. Her brother and I always called her Twig. It's a dumb joke. Their last name is Birch, and she was tall and skinny as a kid, and the younger sister always trying to see what we were up to. Paul always called her Twig, I guess, and I just picked up on it. I'm sure we said it to annoy her. It just stuck in my head."

"Adorable," Edgar kidded. "So you just hung out at their house all day?"

"Nah, just for dinner, and then Emma and I stopped off at the pub for a drink before she came to work here."

"Oh, a drink, huh? Okay."

"What's that supposed to mean?"

"I'm just kidding you, man." Edgar laughed. "It's just not something you really do, is all. Ray is the big player hooking up in every city we go to, and I know

Pete and I have had our fair share over the years. Hell, even Jordan scores with some of the older chicks who hang around after shows. You usually shy away from that stuff, at least as we have gotten older."

"That shit gets old, Eddie. It was flattering when we were young, but I got over that years ago. It's more of a headache than anything else. Figuring out how to slyly dislodge yourself from somebody different each morning is a hassle. Then you have to worry about who she will tell, whether she takes pictures or video, where it will end up, and who knows what else. So it's not worth it."

"I get it. Do your own thing, Noah. We're going to be here for a couple of more days anyway without our equipment. You want to hang out with this woman, I say go for it. The rest of us might go a little stir-crazy sitting around this hotel with nothing to do. Ray is going to kill poor Cecil if this lasts too long."
"I can talk to Ray and see if I can calm him down. I'm not sure there's much else I can do. Emerald Lake isn't packed full of activities, but I'm sure we can all get out to do something, anything, to keep busy until the roads are cleared."

"I'm sure Cecil will appreciate that." Edgar nodded as he rose from the bed. "I'm gonna go see what Pete and Jordan are up to. Jordan grabbed his PlayStation from the bus to kill time. Want to join me? I'm sure we can take them in some *Call of Duty*."

"Nah, I think I'm just going to turn in and get some sleep. You go ahead," Noah replied as he stripped off his shirt.

"Maybe you can show me where to get some breakfast around here in the morning then," Edgar asked.

"I would, but I already made plans with Emma when she gets off work at seven."

"Yeah, she's just the sister of an old friend after all. Not the guy you travel around with three hundred days out of the year," Edgar ribbed.

"Both my points exactly!" Noah exclaimed. "I see your ugly mug all the time. If you want to get up at seven and join us, you're more than welcome."

"Fat chance," Edgar said as he moved to the hotel room door. "Give Twig a kiss for me," Edgar joked as he left.

Noah stripped off his jeans after Edgar left and lay on the bed. He grabbed the TV remote and flipped on the local news channel, putting the captions on so he didn't have to turn the volume up. The news showed piles of snow everywhere and road blockages heading north and south of Emerald Lake.

Noah propped some pillows behind his head as he sat up and grabbed his journal from the nightstand. He flipped to the first blank page and stared at it for a moment before writing *Emma* at the top of the page.

Noah's pencil sat poised at the top line, ready to move at his command, but nothing came to him. He prodded his brain to do something, anything, but all he could do was press the point harder into the page, leaving a deep indent the size of a period and nothing more.

****

The empty water glass clunked to the floor, jarring Noah awake from his slumber. He found his journal and pencil lying on the floor as well, having fallen from his lap not long after he had dozed off for the night. Noah groggily rose from the bed, stepping into the damp spot on the carpet the last of his water had left before trudging into the bathroom. He looked himself over in the mirror, giving little thought to his appearance as he yawned before looking down at his watch. He saw it was nearly 6:45 and realized he had just fifteen minutes to get himself ready to meet Emma.

Noah stripped off his clothes in a flash and turned the water on in the shower. He immediately jumped in, the cold water shocking him into a state of alertness. No cup of coffee could perform better.

He washed quickly, forgoing the stubble on his face and darting back to his suitcase to grab what clothes he could to dress for the day. A peek out the curtains revealed hints of the impending sunrise. The sky appeared clearer than it had recently, giving hope to a potentially warmer day without snow.

Noah pulled his boots on to complete his wardrobe and then grabbed the jacket—Paul's jacket—from the chair where he had left it the night before. A chill of unease coursed through his body before he moved out of his room and to the elevators. His watch showed ten minutes after seven, and he hoped that Emma was still waiting for him downstairs.

Noah dodged an older couple just outside the elevator doors when it arrived in the lobby before he hustled toward the front desk. Grace was already at her post for the day, humming along with the Drifters as they sang "White Christmas" over the speakers.

"Good morning," Grace chirped.

"Hi," Noah replied. "Is Emma here?"

"Her shift ended at seven," Grace announced. "Is there anything I can help you with instead?" she asked eagerly.

"No, no, thank you, Grace," Noah said, disappointment tinging his voice.

Noah shuffled his feet and turned around, readying to head back to his room, when he spotted Emma standing by the Christmas tree, her coat draped over her arm.

"I was beginning to think you weren't going to show." She grinned.

"I'm sorry," Noah apologized as he approached the glimmering tree. "I guess I overslept. I didn't set the alarm or anything, and I was trying to write last night—"

"Did you write something?" Emma asked excitedly.

"Nothing," Noah replied. "Anyway, I'm sorry I'm late."

"No big deal," Emma said, brushing it off. "It was nothing set in stone like a date or anything."

The inference caught Noah off guard as he stumbled for words, causing Emma to laugh.

"Relax, Noah," she assured him. "Let's go. Talk to you later, Grace."

Grace watched on as Noah walked to the front door, pulling it open so Emma could walk outside.

"How was your night?" Noah said as they sidestepped some rapidly dripping icicles over the awning at the entrance to the hotel.

"Pretty quiet, I guess," Emma said as she strolled along. "Your friends called down a couple of times because they needed a few things, but other than that, not much is going on. We have a few more people coming in with reservations today since we're getting close to Christmas. People visiting family and all, you know."

"I hope Ray isn't too much of a pain in the ass for you," Noah quipped. "He can be a bit demanding."

"It's okay. I'm used to demanding guests. After the first night, I try to anticipate so I don't have to run around too much. But, of course, it was Cecil who did all the running back and forth to get stuff for him more than anything else."

"Yeah, Cecil is a saint for putting up with Ray's BS," Noah replied.

Noah took Emma's arm and guided her around a slush puddle on the sidewalk as they approached the diner's entrance.

"Do you want to stop in for some breakfast?" he asked.

"How about we go back to the house, and I make breakfast for you?" Emma answered.

"You just worked all night. I don't want you to have to do that."

"I really don't mind at all. In fact, I love doing it. It helps get rid of some pent-up energy after I get home so I can sleep better. Come on."

Emma stepped a little faster, so she was ahead of Noah before he worked to catch up. They eased past the front window of the Birch Tree.

"I just have to stop in for a sec. Is that okay?" Emma asked as she pulled the door to the store open.

Noah nodded in agreement and followed her inside.

"Morning, Dad," Emma yelled, realizing her father was in the stockroom.

"Hey, honey. I'll be out in a jiff," Clay answered.

Emma noticed Mrs. Travers walking toward the front counter, carrying a box of Christmas ornaments. The older woman shakily put the box on the counter before fumbling with her purse a bit. Noah looked on as Emma darted behind the counter.

"Good morning, Mrs. Travers," Emma said loudly.

"Oh, hello, dear." Mrs. Travers smiled. "Where's your father?"

"He's in the back. I can ring you up."

Noah watched as Emma handled the computer register, tallying up the small order.

"Oh, Emma, can you add a bag of rock salt onto that? John was supposed to pick two up for me, and he only got one yesterday."

"Sure thing." Emma smiled, totaling the order and taking payment.

Noah spied the older woman glancing down at the giant bag of rock salt before he dashed over.

"Let me get that for you," Noah said as he picked up the bag and placed it on his shoulder.

Mrs. Travers smiled at Noah, squinting at him.

"Paul? When did you get back?" she croaked.

"No, Mrs. Travers," Emma added politely. "That's not Paul. That's my—my friend, Noah. We can help you out to your car."

Emma snatched up the shopping bag from the counter and went to the front door, jingling the bell as it opened.

"See you later, Dad!" she shouted. "We're helping Mrs. Travers."

"Okay!" Clay yelled. "Wait a minute—we?"

Noah and Emma were already out the door when Noah spotted Clay coming out to the storefront, watching them walk to the sidewalk toward the old Buick parked right out front.

Emma placed the shopping bag on the car's front passenger seat while Mrs. Travers fumbled with the keys to open the trunk for Noah. He politely shifted the heavy load from one shoulder to the other as he waited for the trunk to pop open. Once it rose, he gingerly placed the bag down inside.

"Thank you so much." Mrs. Travers smiled as Noah closed the trunk firmly. "Such a sweet young man." Mrs. Travers pulled two singles from her coat pocket and went to hand them to Noah.

"Oh, no, Mrs. Travers, that's not necessary," Noah insisted, putting his hands up.

"Nonsense, Paul," she fought. "I always tip you for your help."

"You better just take it," Emma whispered as she looked on. "That's not Paul, Mrs. Travers. That's Noah. Paul—Paul isn't here."

Mrs. Travers squinted again through her fogged glasses before taking them off and getting right up to Noah.

"Oh, I'm sorry," the older woman said to Noah, smiling at him. "These damn spectacles do no good. I'm going back to George Bailey and telling him I need new lenses. What a handsome man you are."

"Thank you," Noah said humbly, taking Mrs. Travers's arm and leading her to the driver's side of the car before helping her get in. She started up the car, letting the motor roar before taking the window down to look at Emma and Noah.

"Thank you so much, both of you." She grinned. "Emma, you have a fine young man there. Don't let him out of your sight. I might steal him from you."

Noah glanced at Emma and saw her blushing crimson.

"Have a good day," the elderly woman spoke before spinning her tires loudly and peeling out from the parking space to tear down the street toward home.

"She seems sweet," Noah mentioned as Emma's blush began to fade.

"She's very nice," Emma said as the two started walking again. "Her family has been around Emerald Lake forever. She owns a couple of the big houses around here. Mrs. Travers has been widowed for a long time. John is her caretaker and kind of runs things for her, but she still likes to get out and about. I'm sorry about the Paul thing. She still remembers when he worked at the store. It was probably the jacket that did it."

"Oh, it's okay," Noah brushed it off. "Paul's not a bad guy to get confused with, you know."

"No, no, he's not," Emma agreed.

Noah approached the Birch house, making sure to get the door for Emma to go into the mudroom first. He watched as Emma kicked off her boots and shed her winter coat and hat, hanging them up right away before turning to Noah to take his jacket as well. Noah also dutifully took off his boots, leaving him in just his socks.

"Is that you, Emma?" Noah heard her mother's voice echo from the living room.

"Yes, Mom," Emma yelled back. "Everything okay?"

"Fine, but you didn't call me before you left work."

"I'm sorry, I forgot." Emma sighed, turning to Noah. "Noah walked me home anyway. I'm safe."

"Oh, Noah is here!" she said excitedly. "I'm still in my robe. I look a fright."

"It's okay, Mrs. Birch," Noah said as he sat at the kitchen table.

"Emma, can you help me get back to my room so I can change?"

"Sure, Mom," Emma said with a laugh. "I'll be back in a minute," she whispered to Noah, placing her hand on his arm before quickly pulling it back.

Noah listened as he heard Emma push Alice's wheelchair from the living room down the hall before a distant door closed. Noah scanned the kitchen, found the coffee maker and coffee, set about making some and grabbing some mugs from the cabinet. Once the coffee was underway, he wandered into the living room, where the Christmas tree sat near the fireplace. A small fire showed hot coals going while Christmas music played softly in the background. Noah spied the stockings hanging from the mantle over the fireplace, each hand sewn and stitched with a family member's name on it. At the end of the row was a stocking for Paul.

Noah moved to the end to look at it and saw some framed pictures on the mantle. They looked to be of

Christmases long ago, with Paul as a youngster by himself opening presents, and then one of him sitting with a toddler with flaming red hair that had to be Emma.

"Oops, I didn't know Emma was bringing company home," Hayley said from behind Noah, causing him to spin around. He saw Hayley standing before him in sweatpants and a T-shirt, her blond hair tied back.

"Sorry for the surprise," Noah said as he placed one of the frames down. "I didn't think we were coming here either."

"No prob," Hayley said as she moved toward the kitchen to see if the coffee was ready. "You probably worried Mom more than anything."

"Yeah, Emma went to help her get changed," Noah said.

The two sat in silence for a moment at the kitchen table. Noah felt the intense gaze of Hayley upon him as he searched for something to say.

"So you're graduating this year, huh?" Noah began.

"Yeah, finally," Hayley groaned. "I'll be glad to be done."

"Any college plans?"

"Mom and Dad want me to go to Oneonta, of course." Hayley sighed. "You know, the whole family tree and everything. But me, I want to go out west. I already have volleyball scholarship offers from UCLA and Long Beach State."

"Wow, that's impressive. Good for you."

The slow drip of the coffee into the coffee pot cut through the muffled singing of Bing Crosby in the background.

"What about you?" Hayley asked, plucking a banana from the bowl on the table.

"What about me? School passed me by a long time ago," Noah answered.

"No, I meant what are you going to do? Is the Diagnosis thing still going, or are you moving on? No offense, but you guys don't exactly burn up the radio or streaming."

"Ouch, don't hold back or anything," Noah said, feeling the sting. "I mean, I know Emma didn't know who we are but—"

Hayley let out a laugh.

"Don't go by Emma when it comes to anything contemporary," Hayley said as she peeled the banana. "She'd be hard-pressed to tell you the name of anything that has happened in the last ten years. It's just the way it is with her. We all say she has an old soul. She'd rather sit around reading an old book or baking than going out on a Saturday night."

"So, I guess that means she doesn't have a boyfriend or anything," Noah stated, trying to sound casual.
The moment the words escaped his mouth, he saw Hayley grin widely.

"Emma? A boyfriend? No, she doesn't. In case you haven't noticed, we live in Mayberry North here. Everyone knows everyone else's business here, and the pickings are pretty slim for a single girl in her twenties. So it's just another reason for me to go to California. I never understood why Emma stuck around during and after college. She could have gone anywhere. Why the curiosity?"

"Oh, well, I don't know," Noah fumbled. "I guess that you know she's smart and funny, and pretty. I figured she would be with someone, is all."

"You got all that from seeing her for two days after not seeing her for ten years, huh?" Hayley smiled as she bit the banana.

"I think the coffee is made," Noah answered, standing up to pour a cup.

"Nice dodge, rock star," Hayley scoffed as she tossed her banana peel into the trash can and held out an empty mug for Noah to pour coffee into. "Don't worry. I won't tell Emma."

"Tell me what?" Emma asked as she walked into the kitchen, grabbing her Christmas-themed apron off the hook on the wall.

"Nothing, really," Hayley said as she sat down with her coffee. "Noah here was just asking me some questions about the town and its dating prospects for you."

Noah froze in his tracks before he sat. He caught a glimpse of Emma staring at her sister with her mouth slightly open.

"What?" Emma asked. "Why—why would anyone care about that, anyway? Nothing is going on around here," Emma said, pushing the topic aside. Noah sat back at the table and scowled at Hayley.

"That's what I said," Hayley told her sister. "I mean, unless you count Alan Embree."

"Ugh, Hayley, don't bring him up," Emma said as she pulled out a container of flour.

"Who's Alan Embree?" Noah asked Hayley.

"He's a local police officer who's always trying to date Emma. A natural muscle head. He works out in his garage when he isn't on a shift. In the summer, he leaves the garage door open so everyone can watch him with his shirt off. He even grunts extra loud when he sees girls walking by. How many times has he asked you out, Em?"

"Too many to count," Emma said as she began to whisk ingredients together. She then cracked eggs with authority, tossing the shells into a smaller bowl nearby. "He's harmless, mostly. He's just not my type."

"You have a type?" Noah inquired. He watched as Emma began to whisk more aggressively after his question fell into the air.

"We all do, don't we?" Emma dodged. "I'm sure you do too. You just know when you meet that person." Emma turned and caught Noah's eyes with hers.

Hayley lightly coughed to break the spell between Noah and Emma.

"So what are you two up to this morning besides breakfast?" Hayley asked.

"I was hoping maybe to walk around town for a while, perhaps go over toward Emerald Lake and see it, pick up some lunch, anything that gets me out of the hotel room for a while," Noah said, sipping his coffee.

Emma dolloped pancake batter onto the hot griddle on the stove, causing a sizzle immediately.

"Sure, that sounds like fun," Emma replied, adding a few more pancakes.

"I'm sure Mom will love to do that," Hayley tossed in.

"What?" Emma said, spinning around. Noah's eyes darted between the two sisters, wondering if an argument was brewing.

"Well, you usually take Mom on Wednesdays, don't you?" Hayley stated. "I talked about going with Brandi and Ashley for the afternoon."

"Seriously, Hayley? You can't do me a favor this one time?"

"I don't know, Em..." Hayley trailed off, pulling her knees up onto her chair as she drank her coffee.

"It's okay," Noah interrupted. "I'm sure we can do something with your mom."

Emma moved over to the table and stood in front of him. She handed Noah a black spatula.

"Can you watch the pancakes while I talk to my sister?" she asked through a forced smile.

"Sure," Noah replied, gripping the spatula. Emma grabbed Hayley by the wrist, hoisting her out of her chair, and dragged her into the dining room.

Noah walked over to the pancakes, unsure how to tell when each was done or ready to be flipped. He could hear muffled voices sniping back and forth at each other, with the occasional raised voice shouting things like "No way" or "Please?"

Noah placed a couple of the pancakes that looked done onto the white platter next to the stove. He was just about to ladle more batter onto the griddle when the sisters reappeared in the kitchen, with Alice trailing behind in her wheelchair.

"Okay," Emma said, brushing red hair from in front of her eyes. She took the spatula from Noah's hands and reclaimed her position at the stove.

"Could you grab the butter from the fridge?" Emma asked Noah, providing no hint of how the conversation with Hayley went. Hayley had slumped into her chair while Alice took up her customary space at the table.

"Everything okay?" Noah asked with trepidation.

"Perfect," Emma said, attempting to brush off the flour that pocked her black dress pants. "Mom, Hayley is going to spend the day with you. She'll take you out wherever you want to go, and then you guys are meeting Dad for lunch. Sound good?"

"Oh, that sounds nice," Alice replied with a smile. Hayley gave a forced grin to her mother and then turned back to Emma.

"And Emma will be doing my laundry for the next two weeks," Hayley announced.

Noah happily sat and ate breakfast with the Birch women, stealing glances at Emma throughout the meal as they all enjoyed the pancakes, crispy bacon, and homemade English muffins that Emma presented. Once he was stuffed full on breakfast, Noah pushed his plate away.

"I don't think I have eaten that much for breakfast in years," Noah said, running the last of his English muffin through the crumbs of bacon on his plate to polish it all off.

"I'm glad you enjoyed it," Emma said. She rose from the table and started gathering plates.

"No, let me clean up. You cooked," Noah insisted, grabbing the plates.

"It's not a big deal. Hayley can help me," Emma said, looking at her sister.

"Sorry, sis," Hayley said as she stood up. "I need to get ready to take Mom out, remember? I'm sure you can handle it."

Hayley dashed off from the table and ran upstairs before Emma could reply. Noah took the initiative and grabbed the plates back from Emma.

"It's fine," Noah insisted. "I know how to load the dishwasher and wash a couple of pots and pans, Twig."

Alice burst out in a giggle.

"I haven't heard anyone say that in years!" Alice exclaimed. "I forgot they called you Twig. It was always so cute."

"Yeah, adorable," Emma grumbled.

"Oh, don't be like that, Emma," Alice scolded. "You used to like it."

"I was just a kid back then, Mom," Emma retorted. "I'm not twelve anymore. It was different when Paul—"Emma stopped herself from continuing and looked at Noah.

"I'm sorry. I didn't mean to bring up anything like that," Noah said as he mindlessly placed cutlery and plates in the empty dishwasher.

"No, it's okay," Emma said as she reached for the stainless steel pan she had used for bacon. Noah shut the dishwasher and saw Emma drop the pan quickly.

"Shit!" she yelled, sending the pan clattering on the floor as she gripped her right wrist.

"Are you okay?" Noah said, hurrying over and taking Emma's hand in his so he could examine her fingers. He noticed signs of redness on the tips of her index finger and thumb.

"Here," he said, turning on the cool water and holding Emma's hand under the running water. Noah glanced at Emma's face and saw the concern wash away. He gently ran his fingers over hers, checking to see if any blisters were forming before he shut the water off.

Holding Emma's hand once again, he had it up closer to his face, pressing his thumb softly on the pads of her fingers. His eyes met hers, and he noticed a smile come across her face as she broke her gaze from his.

"Thanks," she offered.

"Of course."

"You should go get yourself changed before you two go out," Alice interrupted, pointing to Emma.

"Is—is that okay?" she said, looking down at her clothing covered in flour dust.

"Go, I got this," Noah answered, turning back to the sink and starting on the dishes while whistling "Oh, Christmas Tree."

8

Emma raced upstairs to her room and began to rummage around for clean clothes to change into. Realizing she didn't have time to jump in the shower, she quickly grabbed some undergarments and changed into a pair of blue jeans before searching around her room for her favorite red sweater. She looked through her drawers, closet, and even her hamper but couldn't find it anywhere.

"Hayley!" she yelled, knowing her sister could hear her in her bedroom just down the hall. Hayley sauntered to Emma's door and pushed it open to see Emma bent over the bottom drawer looking through it.

"You bellowed?" Hayley said, standing in the doorway.

Emma peered over at her sister. "Do you have my red sweater?"

"Let me fill you in on a few things Em," Hayley began. "First, you're about five inches taller than me. Second—no offense—but I don't think my girls could be contained in your sweater. It would wear like a crop top. Come to think of it, that might like cute—"

"Hayley!" Emma yelled in frustration. "Can we focus on me for a second?"

"Geez, don't get your panties all in a twist," Hayley said, walking over to Emma's closet. "If you would just relax for a minute, you would see that it's right here."

Hayley climbed onto the small stepstool in Emma's closet and reached up to the top shelf before grabbing the sweater and pulling it down. She tossed it to Emma, who held it up in front of her before slipping it on.

"You're going to wear that?" Hayley questioned.

"Why, what's wrong with it?"

"Nothing at all," Hayley admitted. "It looks great on you. It's just actually something… sexy that you own."

Emma glanced at her figure in the mirror and saw the sweater fit and clung to her nicely with a deeper V-neck than anything she typically wore.

"It doesn't work really well, though," Hayley stated bluntly.

"Gee, thanks. What's wrong with it? You just said it was sexy."

"I mean, it could be sexy if you weren't wearing a sports bra underneath. But come on, Em, you must have something nicer than that."

Emma went back into the top drawer, reaching toward the back before pulling out a black lace bra that still had tags on it.

Hayley snatched the bra from Emma's hands and examined it.

"When did you get this? I've never seen you wear it."

"I've never worn it," Emma admitted. "I bought it a year or so ago, in case I ever—"

"Wanted someone to see it?" Hayley grinned.

"That's not what I was going to say," Emma shot back as her face reddened. She grabbed the garment back from her sister.

"You don't buy black underwear unless you want people to see that you have black underwear, Emma," Hayley said.

Emma stripped out of her sweater and sports bra, removed the tags from the new bra, and put it on. She looked at herself in the mirror, admiring her form, as Hayley walked over behind her. Her sister fixed the straps before reaching around the front and adjusting the bra cups, so Emma's cleavage was more visible.

"Jesus, Hayley, stop!" Emma said, turning around to face her sister.

"You wear a push-up to push things up, Emma. That's all I was doing. Trust me, Noah will notice."

Hayley held out the red sweater, and Emma pulled it on. She admitted that Hayley was right—she was showing more of herself than she ever did, and it made her feel incredibly sexy. A smile crossed her face as she examined her silhouette and then the front.

"You want makeup?" Hayley asked.

"No, I don't wear it," Emma said emphatically.

"Let me at least help you with your hair," Hayley said, guiding her sister out of the room and down the hall to Hayley's bedroom so she could sit at the vanity there.

"You don't have to do this, you know," Emma said as Hayley took out Emma's ponytail and began to brush her sister's red hair.

"Oh, I know. I want to," Hayley answered sincerely. "It's kind of nice to do this with you. We never did anything like this."

"What do you mean?"

"I mean 'sisterly' stuff like this," Hayley replied as she kept brushing. "The age gap always kept us from doing stuff like that. By the time I was becoming a teenager, you were off at college. By the time you finished, I had already done all the stuff myself. So I feel like we kind of missed out on all of it. You know—hanging out, staying up all night listening to music, talking, gossiping, talking about boys—all of it."

"I never thought you wanted to do any of that stuff with me," Emma admitted. "You know, because we're so different."

"We're not so different," Hayley answered, looking at Emma's face in the mirror as her hands rested on her head. "We have a lot more in common than you think."

"I just mean that, I don't know, I guess I was always a little jealous of you," Emma confessed.

"Me?" Hayley laughed as she went and grabbed her curling iron. "Why would you be jealous of me?"

"Everything has always come easy to you, Hayley. Your looks, making friends, schoolwork, social activities, dating—you name it. You always succeeded without much effort. I had, and still have, trouble with all of it. I think it makes me resent you."

"Huh," Hayley said. "And here I was jealous of you the entire time."

Emma watched as curls formed and each part of her hair as Hayley worked.

"You have no reason to be jealous of me, trust me," Emma spouted.

"Not true, Emma. Sure, some of the stuff you mentioned was a little easier for me, but it's just confidence. You have it, but you need to let it out more. I've always been jealous of your relationship with Mom and Dad."

"What are you talking about? They love you as much as me."

"Oh, I know that. But they respect you more than me. Mom and Dad treat you differently, and you can't deny it. When they look at you—well, I think they see more of Paul in you than in me."

Emma stared back at her sister in the mirror. Then she reached her right hand up and placed it on Hayley's left hand.

"I had being the oldest child thrown at me out of nowhere, Hayley. I think Mom and Dad needed me to be more responsible than a fourteen-year-old might typically be, so I just did it. It didn't have anything to do with how they felt about you."

Hayley nodded, then put her hands on the sides of Emma's head and fluffed out the shoulder-length curls she had created.

"What do you think?" Hayley asked.

Emma gazed at her reflection and smiled. "I can't believe that's my hair." Emma spun out of the chair and faced her sister.

"Noah would have to be blind not to notice you." Hayley laughed.

"I didn't do all this to—" Emma started.

"Oh, stop," Hayley said, holding up her hand. "You've been tripping over yourself since he walked in the house yesterday. There's no denying it, Emma. It's okay to like him, you know. He's handsome as hell, a musician, and a nice guy. The fact that he's single is a miracle. Besides, he's into you."

"You think?"

"There's no doubt about it," Hayley said firmly. "The way you two keep making eyes at each other is sickening. Come on, the guy got up at seven in the morning to walk you home and spend the day with you. He's interested."

"Thanks. For everything." Emma hugged Hayley, surprising her sister.

"I want details," Hayley said into Emma's ear. "All of the messy ones."

"Oh, stop," Emma said, breaking the hug. "We're probably just going to walk around town, get some lunch, and that's it. There won't be any messy details."

"Well, that's disappointing," Hayley huffed.

Emma walked out of her sister's room and back to hers to make sure she grabbed her cell phone. Before she could turn and go, Hayley stopped her in the doorway and gave her a gentle push back into her room.

"What?" Emma said with annoyance. "I need to get going."

"I just thought you should have this before you go anywhere," Hayley said and handed her sister several packages of foil.

"Really, Hayley?" Emma chided, just above a whisper.

"Hey, you never know how things are going to go," Hayley added. "I'm just making sure you're prepared for all possibilities. If you don't want them—"

Hayley went to take the condoms back, but Emma held them tightly.

"No, wait," Emma said, looking down at her hand. She slowly pulled the packages back and stuffed them into the back pocket of her jeans.

"Thatta girl!" Hayley smirked.

Emma bounded down the steps before she had a chance to change her mind about all of it, including going out for the day with Noah. It meant she would be running on no sleep, but it was a chance she didn't want to pass up.

Upon reaching the bottom step and turning to the living room, she saw Noah helping push her mother's wheelchair to her usual spot with the best view of the fireplace, the Christmas tree, and the front window. Noah looked in her direction, his eyes catching hers. She followed his sightline as it worked its way down her body and back up again, giving her a secret thrill.

"All set?" Emma asked as she made her way over to where her mother sat.

"I think so," Alice replied, pulling her sweater over her shoulders. "Well, don't you look pretty?"

"Thanks, Mom," Emma said as she bent to give her mother a kiss on the cheek. Then Emma rose and stood in front of Noah as he continued to stare at her.

"You look... great," Noah said softly as if he caught himself.

Emma bashfully ran her right hand through the curls of her hair.

"Thank you," she replied.

"You two have a fun day today." Alice smiled.

Emma began to lead Noah toward the back door before she heard Hayley come up behind them.

"Yes, have a fun day together," Hayley added with a wide grin.

Emma reached over and grabbed Noah by the arm, dragging him toward the back door where their coats hung. She slipped into her boots and grabbed her coat to put it on, and watched as Noah stared at the jacket he had worn—Paul's jacket.

"Maybe I should just grab my coat back," Noah indicated.

"You might want this one if we are going to be outside a lot," Emma told him, grabbing the plaid jacket off the hook. "It's okay, really."

Noah grabbed the garment from Emma and put it on before Emma hustled him out the door. After all the torrential snow of the last several days, the brief respite of the morning gave a warmer feeling to the air and created the beautiful atmosphere Emma enjoyed most about winters in Emerald Lake, especially early in the morning. Icicles clung tightly to eaves and tree branches, not showing the slightest hint of giving way. Even the slightest breeze sent a jingling through the air as the ice rattled, providing a holiday feel only nature could offer.

Emma walked side by side with Noah as they paced back toward the center of town.

"So what would you like to see?" Emma asked.

"It's been a while since I was here. Is there anything of note to look at?"

"That might be a tough one." Emma laughed. "It's Emerald Lake, Noah. Time kind of stands still here sometimes. Some of the small shops you remember might be gone, but they've been replaced by similar small shops, so you might not even notice. However, we did get a pizza place a couple of years ago—Gino's. So that was a big deal. And the town did add a gazebo down by the lake and a bandstand for concerts."

"Let's walk down to the lake," Noah replied. "That was always a fun spot."

Emma's long strides had her moving slightly ahead of Noah as they walked. She relished in the warm sun hitting her face and looking up at the Christmas decorations all through town. When they reached the town hall building, Emma took a moment to admire the tall evergreen they had decorated for the holidays, now adding the snowfall to its boughs to make it look prettier.

"I love the way the town tree looks after it snows," she told Noah. "It's even prettier at night. I can see it glowing as I walk to work at night."

The couple swung past the town hall and made their way just to the edge of the Main Street area where the lake resided. Emma walked down the path toward the lake with Noah following her. A few kids and adults were already out and about walking around the lake, with some diehard runners jogging along the cleared path that circled the area.

"There's the gazebo." Emma pointed to her left at the white covered area with benches underneath. The marquee was decorated with greenery, poinsettias, and wreaths with lights strung along the top. The bandstand stood next to it, but the area was covered in feet of freshly fallen snow.

"Do you want to check it out or go down to the lake?"

Emma watched as Noah stared out over the frozen water, his breath visible in the air.

"Let's go to the lake," he answered, walking farther down the path.

Emma followed behind now, watching Noah pace until they reached the area the town had set up for skate rental. Noah had stopped short of the lake's edge where benches and the covered rental area sat.

"It looks amazing," Noah said quietly.

"It's still the best thing about this town," Emma said proudly.

"I can remember coming down here with Paul in the summers to swim or fish or take the boat out. Then, in the winters, it was down here to skate."

"I remember it too," Emma added. "More often than not, I would try to tag along, and you guys would leave me behind."

"That was Paul," Noah said, attempting to defend himself. "He was funny about that. He always said—"

"I know what he said," Emma cut in. "I don't want little sister Twig getting in the way. I understand. I got that way with Hayley when it was my turn to be the big kid in the family. I just wanted to hang out with you guys because you seemed so cool."

"Trust me, we weren't." Noah laughed. "Paul just wanted to come down here to meet the girls skating. Of course, there was always that one girl—what was her name?"

"Erin Miley," Emma huffed. "She would skate around here in her short skirt all the time. Most of the boys in town came down here to watch her."

"That's right!" Noah exclaimed. "I remember her now."

"Everybody remembers her," Emma added with an eye roll.

"Paul always threatened he was going to ask her out, but I don't think he ever did. I tried to prod him a couple of times, but he just wouldn't do it. He was always too shy. Even when we would go to college parties together, he would back off when we were with the girls."

"I guess he just wasn't the ladies' man you are," Emma jabbed.

"Me? Nah, I really wasn't."

"Somehow, I doubt that, Noah," Emma said as they sat down on one of the benches and watched skaters. "Especially once you were a star."

Emma flipped her hair back with her hand as if she were posing for the paparazzi.

"Yeah, well, it's not really all it's cracked up to be," Noah admitted. "The media likes to make things sound worse than they really are. And I would hardly say I am a star or ever was one."

Emma glanced over to see Noah staring down at the ice and snow at his feet.

"I think you were—I mean, are… a star. You have hit records, songs that play on the radio or get streamed. That's more than most people can say," Emma said.

"I suppose," Noah answered, still looking down.

Emma rose from the bench, determined, and stood in front of Noah.

"Come on," she commanded.

"What?" Noah asked, looking up.

"We're going skating. Come on."

"Emma, I haven't skated in who knows how long—"

"All the more reason to do it," Emma told him. "I'm not missing a day of sleep so you can sit around and mope about how horrible your life is being a musician. Now get up."

Emma held out her gloved hand authoritatively and was a bit surprised when Noah took it.

"Okay." He sighed, standing up.

Emma led Noah over to the skate rental kiosk, and each grabbed a pair of skates. Emma quickly went back to the bench to change out of her boots while Noah lagged behind. He sat, staring at the skates for a moment as Emma already had her first skate laced on.

"What's wrong?" she asked as she began putting on the second skate.

"I don't know," Noah said cautiously. "The idea of putting my foot into skates that who knows how many other people wore doesn't excite me."

"Oh, for crying out loud," Emma complained. "Now you sound like a pampered rock star like your friend Ray. Do you need the crust cut off your sandwiches, and you only want the green M&M's in your bowl?"

"I am nothing like Ray, trust me," Noah said emphatically.

"Then prove it and put your damn skates on," Emma said as she got on the ice and skated backward, away from Noah and farther out onto the ice.

Emma glided around while keeping watch on Noah to see that he started to put the skates on. She skated closer to him as he wobbled his way onto the ice and took a few gentle steps forward to get his feet underneath him.

"I can ask them if they have some double-railed skates for you like the toddlers wear if you want," Emma kidded as she slid next to Noah and circled around him.

"Now I know why Paul was always trying to ditch you," Noah said. "You've got a mean streak."

"Me?" Emma cooed innocently before breaking into a smile.

Emma circled Noah again, keeping her eyes on his as she did before she came to a stop just a foot or two in front of him. Noah struggled to keep his balance but stood still.

"Come on," Emma taunted. "Mr. Webb is out there skating, and he's eighty," she said, pointing to the elderly man striding quickly on the ice. "You're not nearly that old, are you?"

"That's it." He grinned and started to skate toward Emma. Initially, she moved slowly, skating backward, until she realized Noah had gotten his feet underneath him and remembered what he was doing. He began to make rapid movements toward her, causing her to turn and skate forward faster.

"You're not getting away this time," Noah yelled.
"Whatever you say, Grandpa!" Emma shouted back. She let out a lighthearted shriek as she felt Noah's gloved hand just touch the tail of her jacket as she turned. Emma looked back at him and playfully stuck her tongue out.

She noticed Noah grin and squint his eyes as he increased his skating speed, catching up to Emma faster than she expected him to until he was right beside her. Noah reached out to grab Emma's hand, and just as he did, he hit a small divot in the ice, causing him to stumble. Before Emma knew it, Noah's feet came out from underneath him, and he skidded directly into her, knocking her down as well so that she landed on top of him.

Emma heard Noah groan as she bounced atop him, knocking the wind out of him as both slid along the ice before coming to a stop just short of the far edge of the lake. Noah gasped loudly as he tried to catch his breath.

"Noah, I'm so sorry," she said, still on him. "Are you all right?"

Noah nodded, still unable to speak. Emma moved off of him so that she was kneeling next to him now. She placed her hand on him above his diaphragm.

"Try to relax, Noah," Emma told him. "Breathe through your nose and bend your knees. Use your stomach muscles. It will pass in a minute."

Emma watched on as Noah stopped trying to gulp for air through his mouth. She kept her hand on him, pressing against his abdomen as his breathing pace slowed. The strength in his abs showed through even with his coat on, and despite Noah catching his breath and breathing normally, Emma found she didn't pull her hand away from him.

Instead, her face hovered over his as she stared into his eyes.

"I think I'm okay now," he said, coughing lightly.

Noah sat up on the ice next to Emma as she pulled her hand back from his body.

"Well, at least I got you." Noah laughed.

"Yeah, you finally did," she added, forcing a laugh herself.

Emma rose from the ice and skated forward toward where the ice ended and a grassy area began. It was a moment or two before Noah got to his feet and joined her.

"What are you looking at?" Noah wondered as he stared forward through a few gnarled trees.

"That house there." Emma sighed as she pointed forward. "It's one of the old Travers' houses. Mr. Travers owned several in town. Unfortunately, this one is still empty. It was always my favorite of all of them. Mrs. Travers lives outside of town. This one just sits here alone."

"That seems a shame," Noah said. "It looks like a big place."

"Oh, it is," Emma replied excitedly. "It's three floors and has eight bedrooms, a beautiful fireplace and kitchen, and even a parlor for entertaining. The Travers family built it back in the 1920s. It has wood floors everywhere, hand carving on the staircases, and so much artistry throughout the place."

"Sounds very nice," Noah said. "Why's it still empty?"

"I think Mrs. Travers doesn't want to sell it just yet. They never had any children of their own, and it was special to her. I've talked to her a lot about it and was lucky to walk through it with her. I always thought it was the ideal place for—"Emma cut herself before she went any further and began to turn and skate away slowly.

"Ideal for what?" Noah asked as he trailed after her.

Emma turned to face Noah and stopped moving.

"You'll think it's silly," Emma said, shaking her head.

"How do you know if you won't tell me?"

"I always thought it would be the perfect spot for a bed and breakfast—my bed and breakfast," she answered. "I got my degree in hotel management and thought it might be great to run a big place one day in the corporate world. After college, I came home because of Mom and didn't think I would get the chance. But this house," she said, pointing once again, "this house just inspired something in me. I know I can make it beautiful and successful, and it would give me a chance to run a business and do my baking while staying in the town I grew up in."

Emma looked over and saw how Noah was staring at her.

"I know, it sounds like some fairy tale Lifetime movie thing, doesn't it? That's why I don't tell anyone."

"I don't think it's silly at all," Noah said. "We all have dreams, Twig. If I hadn't chased mine, life would have been much different for me. So don't just toss it aside like it doesn't mean anything. There are always possibilities."

"Yeah, well, Mrs. Travers isn't selling anytime soon, and even when she does decide to, I don't think I can afford to come up with the down payment, the mortgage, and do all the repair work it will need to turn into a viable place. It is just a dream."

"I like it," Noah added as he skated closer to Emma. "I'm sure you'll find a way to make it happen. You were always determined, Twig. Hell, you got me to put on a pair of skates today. Anything is possible."

Emma stared at Noah, looking at the thin beard covering his strong jaw, and smiled at him. Her eyes went down his body and scanned his jacket and his jeans.

"Oh, Noah, you're soaked from the ice," she exclaimed.

"Yeah, I guess I am," he lamented, running his hand over the back of his jeans.

"We should get you back to the hotel so you can change," Emma stated as she began to skate toward the rental kiosk, trying to tow Noah along with her. He eventually caught up, so he was side by side with her and continued to hold on to her hand, bringing a smile to her face.

Once they got their boots back on, Emma made sure they both stepped rapidly toward the hotel so Noah could change. The hotel stood on the opposite of the street of the lake, so the walk to the lobby took no time at all.

Emma held the front door open as Noah shuffled through, his pants starting to freeze lightly, causing him to walk bow-legged like a cowboy and elicit giggles from Emma.

"I'm glad you're so amused," Noah teased as he waddled farther into the hotel.

"Oh!" Grace yelled from behind the front desk, hustling over toward Noah. "Are you all right? What happened?"

Emma appeared through the door, still giggling. She halted when she spotted Grace standing next to Noah.

"Oh, hi, Emma," Grace stated with some confusion. "I didn't know you were working this morning."

"I'm not," Emma replied. "I was just out with Noah—I mean, Mr. Healy, showing him around town."

"We had a slight mishap at the lake," Noah interrupted.

"The lake?" Grace questioned. "You didn't fall through the ice, did you? Should I call the doctor or nine-one-one?"

"No, no, it's nothing serious," Noah reassured. "I just need to change, is all. Thanks for your concern."

Noah began to move toward the elevator while Emma stood frozen in her spot, unsure of what to do.

"You coming, Twig?" Noah asked, shattering the spell that held Emma's staring at Grace.

"Twig?" Grace asked.

Emma said nothing in reply and just moved toward Noah and hopped in the elevator as soon as the doors opened. She prayed the doors would shut before Grace would come over and try to get in or ask more questions.

The doors slid shut, and Emma let out an exhale as the elevator moved.

"You okay?" Noah asked.

"Yeah, I just—I don't know. I'm not sure how Grace is going to react to all that."

"All what? We were just hanging out."

"I know, but we were alone, doing stuff together, and now I'm riding up to your room. I don't know. Grace has an active imagination."

"I think you're worrying too much about it," Noah said as the doors opened to the third floor and he stepped out of the elevator. He turned to face Emma, who hesitated a moment before seeing Noah offer his hand to her to lead her out. Finally, she reached across, and Noah gripped her fingers, tugging her along.

Emma floated along behind Noah as they reached the door to his room. She glanced up at the positions in the hallway where she knew the security cameras were, wondering if Grace or anyone else was watching her. Once Noah opened the door with his card key, she walked in directly behind him, leaving the camera's prying eye behind.

Emma rarely stepped foot into any guest rooms unless they needed help in prepping rooms for guests. The odd taboo feeling that overcame her strengthened more as Noah took off his jacket and kicked his boots off before pulling his shirt over his head, leaving him bare-chested. Emma held a slight gasp in her throat as she saw the well-defined muscles that had been hidden from view, along with a couple of glimpses of the tattoos Noah wore. It certainly wasn't the body she recalled seeing when they swam at the lake, and she was a teenager gawking at Noah and Paul.

"Take your coat off and relax," Noah told her.

Emma nodded and shed her coat, hanging it on the back of the door and revealing the low-cut sweater she had decided to wear. Noah rose from the chair and headed off toward the bathroom, leaving the door ajar. The telltale sound of a belt buckle being undone and then hitting the porcelain tile echoed through Emma's ears as she felt her face redden. She caught a peek at Noah through the barely-opened door, standing in his navy blue boxer briefs before Noah looked up at her, causing her to spin around and look at the mirror, where she found she could still see him.

"Twig, can you reach into the drawer there and grab another pair of jeans for me?" Noah asked.

"Sure," she said, her hands shakily going to the dresser and pulling a pair of black jeans from the top drawer.

When Emma looked back up in the mirror, she gasped again when she saw Noah's reflection right behind her.

"Sorry, I didn't mean to startle you," Noah said.

"It's okay," she said softly. "I just... didn't expect to see you there... wearing, well..."

"Oh, I apologize," Noah said, grabbing the jeans from Emma. "I'm so used to dressing and undressing in front of who knows who. I guess I don't even think about it anymore."

"I guess," Emma said with a forced laugh.

"I mean, we've seen each other in bathing suits and all," Noah said. Emma watched as his eyes went from hers down her body, his view drinking her in.

"That—that was a long time ago," Emma answered, her throat getting drier.

"It was," Noah agreed. "We're both different now."

Noah stepped even closer to Emma, leaving sparse inches between the two of them as he came face to face with her. The intensity of his gaze proved too much for her as she went to look down. Within seconds, she found Noah's index finger on her chin, tilting her face back up to his.

Before Emma could react or say anything at all, Noah leaned in and pressed his lips to hers.

9

The impulse to kiss Emma seemingly came from nowhere for Noah. What had started as an innocent outing for breakfast and to see the town became much more as the morning pressed on. Noah had difficulty concentrating from the moment he spotted Emma emerge in her red sweater and jeans. She was far from the girl he remembered from years ago, and the conversations they had the night before and all morning only increased his feelings for her.

Noah noticed some reluctance from Emma when he first went to kiss her. He broke his lips from hers gently and earlier than he wanted to.

Emma took a small step back from him, bringing her hand up to her lips before looking at Noah. Emma was one of the few women Noah had met that he could look eye to eye because of her height.

When Emma hesitated with saying anything or reacting in, Noah stepped closer to her again.

"I'm sorry. I didn't mean to catch you off guard like that. It just… I wanted to do that since the moment we were on the ice together."

A blush rose to Emma's cheeks as she gave Noah a small smile. She stepped closer to him, her body nearly pressed to his, and she placed her hands on his cheeks before kissing him. Noah put his hands on Emma's waist and held her as he took his time kissing her this go-round before Emma gently moved her head back to take a breath.

"I guess you were okay with it." Noah smirked.

"Uh-huh," Emma whispered, pressing against Noah's bare chest.

It was all the assent Noah needed to hear. Before Emma could do anything else, Noah scooped her up in his arms and carried her the short distance to the king-sized bed, placing her down in the center. He positioned himself on the bed so he could pull her boots off, revealing the fuzzy Christmas socks she wore. His hands snaked up to Emma's calf to remove the first sock. She let out a loud giggle as he tugged the last bit off and grazed his index finger along the sole of her foot before doing the same to her right foot.

Noah slid up on the bed so he was at Emma's side, facing her before he placed his palm on her right cheek and went back to kissing her. The kissing was more passionate now, with no hesitation from either of them. Noah's lips hungrily moved from Emma's to the nape of her neck, his fingers entwining in her red hair as he did so. His arousal was evident in his boxer briefs, and he draped his left leg over to Emma's, pulling her more to her side and pressing against her in her denim.

Noah's left hand moved over Emma's body, tracing the outline of her breast in her sweater before he reached the bottom of it. Then he deftly began to lift it, sliding his hand across the warm skin of Emma's belly and up until it reached her lace-covered breast. The base of his thumb swept across her nipple, and Emma let out a light moan that Noah smothered with yet another kiss.

His hands now furiously worked the bottom of the sweater so that he could lift it over Emma's head, breaking their kissing briefly so Noah could remove the garment. Emma wasted no time at all and unhooked the bra, shrugging it from her shoulders and tossing it aside so Noah could feel her bare chest pressed to his. His lips went to work on her neck and shoulders as Noah noticed Emma's hands moving across his chest to his abs before her hand dipped down to his briefs and fondled him.

Noah rolled to his left, so he was atop of Emma, looking down at her. He began to kiss his way down from her lips and neck to the gap between her breasts. Emma's hands held tightly to his hair as Noah moved, keeping him in place as his lips reached for the most sensitive areas of her breasts. She released her grip on his hair as he continued moving downward, his hands resting at her hips before his left hand moved over, undid the button of her jeans, and eased the zipper down.

A few slight tugs on the pants led to Emma rapidly forcing her pants to the bottoms of her feet before she could kick them away and Noah could resume exploring her body. Noah trailed his fingertips along the insides of Emma's thighs, bringing about goose bumps and light moans simultaneously. Next, he hooked his index fingers inside the delicate lace of her panties and eased them down her legs until they were off. Noah reached down and pulled off his briefs, freeing his erection before he stopped himself.

"What's wrong?" Emma panted. "I'm beyond the teasing point, Noah," she said hungrily.

"No, no. It's not that," Noah added, trying to control himself. "Believe me, I want to. I'm just trying to remember where I might have a—"

Emma let out a laugh, bringing her hand to her face.

"This is embarrassing," she started. "Check the back pocket of my jeans."

Noah climbed off the bed and picked up the pants, rummaging through the pockets before he discovered several foil packets there. He held up the condom packets for Emma to view and smiled at her.

"I swear to you, I did not plan this," she offered. "Oh, God, this is humiliating."

"Twig, it's fine," Noah said soothingly. He ripped one of the packages open with his teeth, pulled the condom out, and rolled it on. "I don't really care why they were there right now."

Noah got back on the bed, kissing his way up Emma's left thigh before positioning himself over her. He watched her eyes as her tongue lightly rolled across her lips. As he eased inside her, Emma's eyes widened before closing completely. She groaned at each one of Noah's moves, and Emma raised her knees slightly so that Noah could go deeper into her. He plunged his cock in, holding steady before slowing moving back out, over and over, until Noah noticed Emma was gripping the sheets beneath her tightly in each of her fists.

"Noah, please," Emma begged, her eyes barely slits as she looked up at him as he thrust forward.

Noah increased his pace, getting closer and closer himself, his body grinding along with Emma's until he felt her thighs tighten around him as she moaned.

"Right there. Don't stop," she pled loudly, her arms wrapping around Noah's neck.

Noah had no intention of stopping as they both teetered on the edge. One deep push propelled Noah and Emma forward as Emma cried out when she came. Noah moved his head down to Emma's shoulder as her pussy contracted on him, bringing about his orgasm. He groaned deeply into Emma's shoulder, moving to kiss her shoulder and neck as both experienced waves of pleasure through their bodies.

Emma's arms draped themselves around Noah, holding his body tightly to hers so that he could not pull away from her. He kissed her gently over and over. Every time he went to pull away from her, Emma pulled him back.

"Not yet," she whispered in his ear, nibbling on his lobe. "Stay longer."

"I don't want to hurt you, lying on you like this," Noah admitted.

"Trust me, it doesn't hurt at all." She grinned as she wriggled her hips against Noah's.

****

Not long after her first experience with Noah, the two of them drifted off to sleep in Noah's bed. Emma was spent physically after having been up all night working and then spending the day with Noah. However, as soon as he offered to lie next to her with her head on his shoulder, she found herself sound asleep. She couldn't remember the last time she had felt so relaxed, safe, and happy.

Emma felt Noah's shoulder slowly pull away from her to the opposite of the bed. She pried her eyes open to see his naked form, first sitting and then standing, and smiled.

"Where are you sneaking off to?" Emma purred, rolling over, so she was on her stomach, arms crossed on the pillow beneath her.

Noah turned to face Emma, surprised she was awake.

"No, not sneaking at all." He smiled back. "I didn't want to wake you. I know you're usually asleep this time of day. So I was just going to jump in the shower."

Emma stretched and yawned, arching her back like a cat that just woke up before looking at Noah again.

"What time is it?" she asked.

Noah plucked his phone off the nightstand to check.

"It's three o'clock," Noah told her.

Emma sat upright in bed.

"I guess I slept longer than I thought I did. So it's that late already?"

"Well, we didn't just sleep." Noah smiled, causing Emma to blush. "But, yeah, it's three. Is that a problem? Do you need to go?"

Emma saw the disappointment on Noah's face.

"No," she replied. "No, I don't. Go take your shower. I'll be right here waiting for you."

Emma crawled off the bed and grabbed the T-shirt Noah had been wearing, slipping it on. The shirt came down to the tops of her thighs, still leaving her a bit uncovered. She reached to pick up the black panties Noah had tossed aside earlier.

"You don't have to put those back on yet if you don't want to," Noah said as he stood naked in the bathroom doorway, clearly watching Emma's every move and enjoying it.

"Fair enough." She laughed, balling the underwear up in her fist before she got back on the bed.

Emma's eyes followed Noah into the bathroom. She heard the shower turn on, and the urge to follow him in was intense. It was only the ding of her cell phone that distracted her from her mission.

Emma reached for her jeans, grabbing the phone from her pocket to see a message from Hayley.

Are you having fun? Or are you at home already?

Emma grinned and typed a message back to her sister.

I'm not home and having fun. Thank you, thank you, thank you for the gift before I left.

She added a smiley face emoji with devil horns to the message and sent it.

Hayley quickly added a reply.

OMG, Em! You dirty girl!

Emma sat back on the bed smiling before she thought to send another message.

Do you think you can take Mom and Dad out for dinner? I don't know that I'll be home in time. Please!!

The message hung on the screen for a bit, leaving Emma wondering about the answer. Then, finally, she saw the ellipsis on her screen to let her know Hayley was responding. Emma mouthed "Please, Please" to herself several times before the reply appeared.

You will owe me BIG for this, Em. Have fun.

Emma sent several heart emojis back to Hayley before putting her phone down, smiling and hugging the pillow next to her.

A light knock on the door startled Emma, causing her to freeze in place. It was followed up by a louder knock and the familiar words, "Housekeeping!"

Emma recognized the voice as one of the room attendants, Tia. She had not even thought to put the "No service" or "Do Not Disturb" sign on the door when they entered, never imagining they would spend the afternoon the way they had so far.

Emma sprang out of bed, grabbing her panties from underneath the pillow, and worked to shimmy into them when she heard the lock open from the card key and the door open. Emma was just getting the underwear over her backside when Tia walked into the room, her cart in tow.

"Oh, miss, I'm so sorry," Tia apologized, turning away from Emma. After a second, Tia turned around.

"Emma?" she said softly. The shower could still be heard running as Emma looked at her coworker.

Tia approached Emma, standing next to her.

"Isn't this one of the band members' rooms?" Tia asked.

Emma nodded, too mortified for any words to come to her.

"I'm sorry," Tia said again. "Grace told me no one was up here and to come to clean the room. I promise I won't say anything."

"Thanks, Tia," Emma said in a hushed tone as the water to the shower went silent.

Tia smiled and hustled to the door with Emma trailing right behind her. She grabbed the hangtag off the back of the door and went to put it on the front when a hand reached over and stopped her.

She looked up to see one of the other band members standing there, staring at her.

"Hi," the scruffy man said to her with a smile. "Don't tell me. You must be Twig."

"Um, yeah," Emma answered hesitantly. She tugged on the T-shirt, suddenly wishing she and Noah weren't so close in height.

"I'm Edgar," he said politely. "I'm the drummer. I was just coming down to see what Noah was up to. I guess he's busy."

"He's just getting out of the—" Emma fumbled for every word and walked back into the room, wishing she could crawl under the blanket, close her eyes, and wake up again, finding it was all a dream.

"I was really hoping you were going to join me in there," Noah said as he emerged from the bathroom, a towel wrapped around his waist while he used another to dry his hair.

"No, thanks, I showered already." Edgar laughed as he sat on the chair.

"Fuck, Eddie, what are you doing here?"

Noah looked over at the bed and saw Emma under the blanket with it pulled up to her chest.

"Hey, I didn't mean to interrupt anything, honest. I was just checking in on you. I wanted to see if you had dinner plans. Apparently, you have something planned. Ray and Jerry are wondering if you fell off the face of the earth. You haven't returned any of their messages or calls."

"Ray can come down here himself if he has something to ask me," Noah huffed.

"Since we both know that isn't going to happen, you should probably just connect with—"

"No, Eddie," Noah said adamantly. He sat down on the bed next to Emma. Emma noticed his hand go under the blanket, searching for hers. She grabbed hold of his fingers and held it.

"I've spent most of my adult life kowtowing to whatever Ray wants so it didn't ruffle his feathers or upset his delicate sensibilities. If Ray wants to talk to me, he can come to me. As far as Jerry goes, he's probably only calling because Ray is bitching about me. I'll call him if and when I want to."

Edgar raised his hands in submission.

"Don't kill the messenger, man," Edgar added. "You do what you need to do. I'm sure I can find something to eat with Pete and Jared."

"The diner is delicious," Emma piped up out of nowhere, causing both men to turn to her. "Get the meatloaf."

"Thanks, Twig." Edgar smiled.

"Her name is Emma," Noah said defensively.

"Sorry. Emma." Edgar nodded as he rose from the chair. "I'll leave you two alone before he jumps across the room and bites my head off. Nice to meet you formally, Emma."

Emma gave a bashful wave as Noah followed Edgar to the door and shut it.

"I'm sorry about that," Noah said as he got on the bed again, still only wearing a towel. "I didn't mean to put you in that situation."

"It's okay, Noah," Emma said. "It was a little embarrassing, but it's fine. You know, if you need to do something else, I can just go home. It sounds like they need you."

"Trust me, they don't *NEED* me for anything. Ray just wants me to do things to make his life easier. I told you I wanted to spend the day with you, and I mean it. So if you need to go home, I'll go with you."

"Are you sure? I don't want to cause any trouble."

Noah brought his face close to Emma's, brushing a few stray strands of hair from in front of her eyes.

"You're the one thing in my life right now that isn't causing me trouble."

Before Emma reacted, Noah had placed his lips on hers, kissing her softly and drawing her closer to him. A soft sigh escaped her lips.

"I don't have to get back home right away," Emma cooed, peeling back the blanket before tugging on Noah's towel.

10

After spending most of the afternoon and early evening together, Emma knew she had to get home to ready herself for work that evening. However, Noah relentlessly worked on her, attempting to convince her to call in sick or take the night off so they could spend more time together.

"I can't call in sick, Noah," Emma insisted as she pulled her jeans on. "It's bad enough Grace saw me walk in with you and go upstairs. She knows I'm here, and God knows who she'll tell about it. So I should just get going."

"Not without me," Noah replied, climbing from the bed and grabbing his boxer briefs.

"You don't have to do that," Emma answered as she slipped her black bra on and donned her sweater. "It sounds like you have people looking for you anyway."

Emma sat on the bed to put her boots on, but Noah walked over and stood directly in front of her. Her eyes wandered up his muscular legs to the waistband of his boxer briefs and then to his defined abs. Emma couldn't resist sliding her hands across the taut muscles there for her enjoyment.

She let out an audible sigh as she did, and Noah leaned forward, pressing his body to hers, so he was on top of her on the bed. His mouth reached hers to kiss her with zeal and take her breath away.

"Are you sure you want to go?" Noah growled into her left ear. Noah's arousal was evident to Emma now, and she allowed his right hand to slip underneath her sweater.

"Noah, you're making it hard for me to think straight." She gasped.

"You're the one who's making it hard," Noah joked, reaching his hand down to unbutton Emma's jeans. His fingers gingerly dipped to the waistband of her panties, drawing ever closer to slipping inside before Emma's hand moved down to stop Noah.

"Noah, we can't," she said as she placed her hands on either side of Noah's face, so she was looking directly at him. "Come walk me home. We can hang out a bit before I have to go to work."

Noah grinned and moved his lips down to kiss Emma's neck once again. He planted soft, lingering kisses on her, causing Emma to shut her eyes. Her resolve slipped away under Noah's touch.

"Noah, behave," she groaned.

"Don't you know that rock stars are bad boys?" Noah said as he continued kissing. "I am behaving. I'm just behaving badly."

"Yes, you are." Emma gasped as Noah pulled her sweater off her shoulder so he could kiss her there.

Emma worked to clear her mind, smiled at Noah, and quickly placed her hands on his hips and rolled him so she was now on top of him.

"This works too," Noah offered, placing his hands at Emma's waist.

"You're insatiable." Emma grinned back at him.

"I know."

Noah propped himself up on his elbows and looked at Emma.

"I'll stop," he promised. "I don't want to, but I will. I'll take a raincheck."

"Good," Emma said as her hand ran down his bare chest before she stood up. She walked over to the T-shirt on the floor, the one she had worn earlier, and tossed it to Noah.

"Now, get dressed so I can get home and change."

Noah finished dressing, and the two left the room and entered the quiet hallway. Noah approached the elevator and pressed the call button. When the familiar ding signaled the arrival, Emma halted Noah before he could enter.

"We can't take the elevator," Emma stated.

"Why not?"

"Because Grace might still be down there. Or worse, Bernadette will be there waiting for me," Emma explained. "Can we take the stairs and go out the back exit?"

"Sure, if you want," Noah agreed. "It seems silly to me that you're worried about them seeing you. Who cares?"

"I don't want to lose my job. Please?"

Noah nodded, and Emma led him to the stairwell where they could descend. Emma's steps echoed loudly as she paced down with Noah behind her. The faint sounds of Bing Crosby singing "White Christmas" became more prominent as they moved, and when Emma opened the door to access the first floor, the music became louder and more evident.

Emma peered left and right, spotting no one in the hall. Finally, she grabbed Noah's hand and quickly moved with him toward the exit door at the rear of the hotel that led into the parking lot behind the building. Darkness had long settled on Emerald Lake, and the shapes of some snow-covered cars and the lengthy tour bus occupied the back lot.

Emma darted to the side of the building and went to the sidewalk, breathing a sigh of relief as they were free from the hotel. Noah walked alongside her now as they moved past the diner and pub toward Emma's home.

The temperature had dropped from earlier in the day, freezing over whatever had lightly thawed during the warmer day hours. When they moved near the Birch Tree, Emma saw the lights were off, letting her know they had closed for the night. The sign in the store window noted that there were just two days left until Christmas to prod all the last-minute shoppers into action.

"I guess everyone will be back at your house since the store is already closed," Noah lamented.

"No, Hayley was taking them out to dinner tonight," Emma replied as they walked. "Mom doesn't get out too much, so she tries to make the most of the days she gets to roam. They probably won't get back until close to when I leave for work."

"Oh, that late, huh?"

Emma saw Noah's face light up. She reached the top of one of the bushes they were walking by, grabbed some snow in her hand, and tossed it at Noah.

"You need to cool off some!" she yelled as she pelted Noah and dashed off toward her house laughing.

"Hey!" Noah shouted as the snow bounced off his shoulder and sprayed on his face. Emma heard his footsteps coming up behind her as he grabbed her coat and pulled her down into the snow just to the side of the walkway. She squealed as she tumbled into the deep snow.

Noah pressed his body on top of Emma's, kissing her.

"That was a dirty trick," Noah said with a smile, wiping snow from the side of his face.

"All's fair in—" Emma cut herself off before finishing that sentence as she gazed at Noah. He stared down at her, unsure of how to react.

"It was pretty naughty of you," Noah answered, changing the tone back. "I should spank you for it," he said with a Cheshire cat grin.

Emma lifted her head from the snow and gave Noah a kiss on the lips.

"You wish," she purred at him before pushing him off her to send him rolling into the snow next to her.

Emma let out a loud giggle before reaching out to make a snow angel. She stood up, admiring her handiwork. She noticed Noah decided to do the same, moving his arms and legs back and forth to make an angel next to hers. They were close enough where it seemed the two cherubs were holding hands.

Emma walked along the path to the back door, entering the mudroom and shaking the snow off her coat before hanging it up. Noah followed suit, brushing snow off the plaid coat. He went to hang the jacket next to Emma's but then moved it two spaces over to place it where Paul had always put it when he came in.

Emma moved to the stairs and began to ascend, signaling to Noah to follow her. She opened the door to her bedroom and flipped the light on, quickly kicking some dirty clothes on the floor underneath her bed.

"Excuse the mess," Emma said with a blush.

"Twig, if you think this is messy, you're in for a shock if you ever see my apartment," Noah replied. "I basically live out of cardboard boxes and suitcases."

"I don't know. It just feels funny to have someone here in my room. I don't think I ever had a boy up here," Emma said, regretting she said it right away. "Oh, God, I sound like such a teenager."

Emma sat down on the bed as she watched Noah walk around and take in the décor of her room. Noah examined the knick-knacks on her shelves, her high school volleyball and basketball trophies and ribbons, and the rows of books she had in her small bookcase. Finally, Noah paused at Emma's desk, looking at the pictures she had on the shelves and the desk itself, including a couple of pictures of her with Paul.

Emma sat on her hands, still attempting to calm herself as Noah inspected her room. She looked on as Noah plucked the navy blue fabric-covered book from the shelf over her computer, brought it over, and sat on the bed next to her. Emma knew just what the book was before he arrived next to her.

The two silently leafed through the scrapbook that contained pictures from Emma's childhood, including a few photos of when she was first brought home from the hospital. Paul, a proud boy of six, held his newborn sister while he sat on the couch. Emma beamed as Noah flipped the pages, and the two laughed over old photos of birthday parties, summer vacations, holidays, and more.

It wasn't until Noah reached near the back of the book and was about to turn the page that Emma reached across to stop him from looking further.

"You don't want to see these," she insisted, placing her arm over the page. "It was more awkward teen years. I was tall, gangly, had weird bangs, you name it. So let's put this away."

"Oh, come on. Those are the best ones."

Noah moved Emma's hand out of the way, and she protested more adamantly.

"Noah, wait!" she insisted.

Noah had already moved to the next set of pages in the scrapbook. He saw only pictures of him and Paul, photos of him and Paul with Emma, and even a few photos of just Noah. A couple of the images had hearts doodled next to where Noah sat or stood, and the one from a summer when Noah had stayed for a few weeks showed him with his arm around Emma, her head on his shoulders as she looked at him.

"Why wouldn't you want me to see these?" Noah asked.

"Because... because they're super embarrassing, mainly," Emma admitted. "I don't know if you know this, but"—Emma took a deep breath—"I had a massive crush on you when I was younger. So yes, I wanted to hang out with Paul and you and do fun teen stuff, but really, I just wanted to hang out with you so you would notice me."

Emma stared down at the scrapbook, afraid to look up at Noah. His fingers crawled across the page and entwined with hers.

"Hey, look at me," Noah said gently.

Emma turned her eyes up to look at Noah's face.

"I knew," Noah told her. "Paul, being the big brother, always used to brush it off or even jibe me about it, but I knew. Honestly, I thought it was sweet."

"I was convinced you had no idea," Emma replied. "Especially when you started to call me Twig or would go along with Paul about leaving me behind while you guys went to the lake or the movies or for ice cream."

"We were teenage boys full of hormones who thought we were cool." Noah laughed. "We thought all the girls would love us because we were college guys. But, boy, were we wrong."

Noah closed the scrapbook and moved closer to Emma, placing his hand on her thigh as he leaned toward her to kiss her. Emma's heart leaped to her throat as she kissed him back.

"I can't believe I'm kissing you, in my bedroom, after telling you that." Emma smirked.

"No offense, but a kiss in your bedroom is pretty far down on the list of things we have done today," Noah added.

Emma glanced at the alarm clock on her nightstand.

"I need to go take a shower and start getting ready for work," she bemoaned.

"You don't have to, you know," Noah told her, trying to sway her decision.

"Noah, we've already been through this," Emma said as she pried herself away from his embrace to stand up. "I'll be quick about it. Just wait here."

"Why do I have to wait here?"

"Because I want to be able to come back and see you sitting in my room, so I know this isn't a dream." Emma smiled as she walked off toward the bathroom.

****

Noah sat idly in Emma's room while she showered. He looked around once again, toying with the stuffed elephant he found lolling on one of the shelves before he ventured out into the hallway. The sound of the water running in the bathroom was evident, and Noah heard Emma humming as he neared the door. He recognized the tune as "Over the Rainbow" and smiled to himself as he listened for a moment. It was then his attention turned to the closed door at the middle of the hallway.

Noah froze for a moment, unsure of what to do. It had been over ten years since he had gone into Paul's room. He wasn't sure if the family even still considered it Paul's room. It could easily have been converted into an office or other guest room by now.

Noah crept down the hall, the floorboards creaking slightly as he approached the door. He half-expected the door to be locked when he turned the doorknob, but it gave way quickly. He pushed with his fingers so that light from the hallway shone into the room, providing just a shaft of a view into what was in there. He saw that the bed was perfectly made as if waiting for Paul to come home and use it like it was when they came back for breaks.

Reaching to the side, Noah found the light switch and flicked on the overhead light and fan in the room. All the decorations that had hung on the walls when he was younger were long gone, revealing nothing but bare, cream-colored walls. A few cardboard boxes remained stacked up in the far corner, and the dresser opposite the bed sat empty, a layer of dust lining the top of it where a few pictures in frames remained. One was of Paul in his uniform with members of his regiment under a flag at their base in Afghanistan. Another was Paul in his dress uniform, flanked by his parents, Emma, and Hayley, taken in their front yard.

Noah glanced to his left and saw the triangle frame positioned proudly on a shelf, with medals on display. One was the Purple Heart, and the other a Silver Star. Noah picked up the star and examined it, bringing it under the light in the center of the room so he could get a better look.

"I told Mom and Dad we should display that stuff downstairs where others could see it," Emma interrupted, startling Noah so that he fumbled with the case before catching it. He looked over and saw Emma standing there, her red hair damp and flat, dressed in a soft gray robe.

"I'm sorry. I shouldn't have come in here," Noah said as he placed the medal down in its proper place. "I guess I just needed to see it. Part of me expected to see him sitting in here on his bed listening to music when I walked in."

"I know." Emma sighed. "I still have days like that too, and it's been ten years. Something will happen during the day where I'll think of him or see something and say, 'Paul would think that's hysterical,' and want to call him."

Noah's chest became tighter the longer he stood in the room. The air suddenly felt stifling, and he forced himself out of the door and down the hallway to Emma's room. Emma trailed behind him, reaching Noah just as he sat on the bed, gasping.

"Are you okay?" Emma asked with concern.

"I should have been there," Noah mourned.

"Where? In Afghanistan? There was no way to know—"

"No," Noah interrupted. "Before that. I should have been in Oneonta. I never should have dropped out and left him there by himself. Paul wanted to go to school. Fuck, he was bright and a great student. I was the one who didn't belong there. I never wanted to be there. Once the music opportunity came along, I jumped at it. It gave me the perfect out. He tried to talk me out of leaving, and I just blew him off. Then I heard a few months later that he had dropped out as well and joined the Army. I couldn't believe it. Paul wasn't an Army guy. I tried to reach him a few times before he left for overseas, but I was on the road a lot, and we never connected. When he died, I just went numb."

"Noah, it's not your fault Paul left school and joined the Army," Emma said, putting her arm around him. "He did what he thought was right for him. I was surprised too, but you know what? He loved it, and he was good at it. He became a whole different person—more confident, outgoing, strong—you would have been proud to see him. All of his military buddies who came to the funeral told us how great he was, how he had saved lives."

"The funeral," Noah whispered. "I didn't even come to the fucking funeral. He was the best friend I ever had, and I didn't even come to say goodbye or respect him."

"Like you said, you were on the road," Emma answered. "You're too hard on yourself."

"I was in New York when his funeral occurred, Twig." Noah snarled. "I was in goddamn Syracuse. I could have been here. But I was too much of a coward to do it. I was an hour or so away, and I didn't come. I couldn't face it—or you and your family. So I have to live with that. I'm sorry. I'm so sorry."

Emma held Noah as he sobbed on her shoulder. Then, finally, the emotion he had held onto for so long flowed out of him.

"You've been beating yourself up over this for ten years, Noah," Emma said as she held him close. "You need to let it go."

Emma pulled away from Noah and looked at him as he sat, broken.

"I haven't been able to write anything since then," Noah admitted. "My heart just hasn't been in it. Every time I try to start something, all these thoughts jumble in my head, and I can't shake them. It haunts me, Emma. It's not Paul—it's the guilt."

"You can't live your life wondering 'what if' all the time, Noah," Emma told him. "Everything happens for a reason."

"I can't believe that there is a good reason that Paul died," Noah spat out.

"Is it horrible that it happened? Of course it is," Emma explained. "I would give anything to have my brother still here. But he saved people when he died, Noah. There are dozens of people who still have husbands, wives, a parent, or a child because of what he did."

Noah sat quietly, attempting to process what Emma told him despite his instinct to deny it.

"In some way, Paul is the reason you and I got together right now." Her hand moved over to Noah's.

"What?"

"Think about it, Noah. Your tour bus gets detoured to a place you haven't been to in ten years, a place maybe you didn't want to go to at all. You've been struggling with your feelings for a long time, and here you are, back in Emerald Lake. Cecil could just as quickly driven on to the next town, and we never would have seen each other. Something made you seek out my father once you got here. Without all of that, we wouldn't be sitting together here now."

"So you're saying this is all because of Paul? Come on, Emma. You don't believe all that paranormal stuff, do you?"

"I'm not saying that, Noah. I am saying that everything happens for a reason. Call it fate, divine intervention, or whatever, but it brought you here to Emerald Lake again, and at Christmas no less. And I can't begin to express how glad I am it did."

Emma rose from the bed and stood in front of Noah, drawing his head to her so that it rested against the soft robe covering her midsection. Noah wrapped his arms around her waist and held on.

"I'm sorry I laid all of that on you," Noah said, looking up as Emma smiled down at him.

"I'm not," Emma answered. "You've been holding onto that guilt for too long. It was time to let it go."

Emma wiped a tear away from her eye as she stepped back, putting her hands on her hips.

"Now, I need to get dressed for work," she announced, moving to her closet.

Noah sat back on her bed, spying her every move.

"Are you going to sit there and watch me?" Emma said as she pulled out a blouse off the hanger.

"You bet I am." Noah grinned.

Emma went into a faux striptease, twirling around the ends of the belt of her robe, peeling it down her shoulders slightly before pulling open the robe and flashing Noah.

Noah slid to the end of the bed, reaching his hands out for Emma and putting them inside her robe around her bare waist. He opened the robe slightly and began to kiss her soft flesh, starting between her breasts and moving down to her belly. Noah gripped Emma's waist and pivoted around, bringing her down to the bed with her robe open.

He continued kissing her, making a trail down her stomach, slowly moving lower and lower until he was between her thighs. One long kiss at the top of her mound drew a moan from her lips.

"Noah," Emma whimpered.

"I'll stop if you want me to," Noah said, continuing on with his mouth. "All you have to do is ask."

His tongue deftly darted inside her as Emma wriggled on the bed.

"Should I stop?" he offered again.

Emma let out a few small pants before looking down at Noah.

"Don't you dare." She sighed.

11

Not long after their last session, Noah relented and allowed Emma to get dressed for work. He looked on as she put on each item, donning a white bouse and reaching for a black pair of slacks hanging in the closet.

"Why don't you wear that?" Noah asked, pointing into the array of clothing.

"What, the skirt? I never wear them," Emma stated.

"Why not? You have long, beautiful legs. You should show them off."

"I'm glad you think they look good," Emma said, holding the skirt on the hanger. "I just think of the long, gawky legs I've always had."

Noah rose from the bed, moving in front of Emma to look her in the eye. Her blouse dangled down to just above her legs. Noah ran his fingertips up Emma's left thigh, grazing the hem of her bouse and sending chills throughout her body, making her shiver.

"There's nothing gawky about them," Noah growled.

"You've convinced me." Emma sighed, her eyes closed as Noah kissed her neck.

Noah stepped back so Emma could continue dressing, eyeing her as she slipped into the black skirt that came just above her knees. She walked over to the dresser and grabbed a pair of dark tights.

"I'm bringing these," she told Noah. It's going to be chilly out there without them. Emma gave a brief twirl in the center of the room to give Noah a glimpse.

Noah placed his hands on Emma's hips, moving to kiss her when a familiar ding came from Emma's phone on the nightstand. She walked over to take a look at it.

"It's from Hayley," Emma said. "I think she's reached the end of her rope for the day with my parents. They are at the pub. Is it okay if we go over there? She did me several big favors today."

"Sure." Noah smiled.

Noah led the way out of the Birch house, up the pathway, and to the sidewalk. A slight breeze blew as they moved, causing them to step a little faster.

"Now I remember why I never wear skirts to work," Emma said as she hurried along. "Damn, that's cold!"

Noah draped his arm around Emma and moved along faster so that they reached the pub quickly. Upon entering, the crowd immediately turned to look and see who was coming in.

"Nice to have you back," Nick commented as the couple walked in. "Twice in one week, Emma. This must be a record for you."

"It might be," she added.

"Your folks are sitting over there." Nick pointed to a booth in the corner. "I can bring drinks over. "Macallan over ice? For both of you?"

Noah nodded in agreement before looking at Emma for her answer.

"Sure, why not?" Emma answered as she moved toward where her family sat.

Noah followed along, letting Emma slide into the booth next to Hayley before sitting on the end.

"Nice to see you two here." Clay grinned, holding up a brown bottle of beer.

"Did you two have a nice day?' Alice asked.

"It was lovely," Emma replied, grinning widely.

"I bet it was," Hayley chimed in. "We had a great time stopping in every store on Main Street, so Mom could look at everything in every place and talk to everyone. Then it was a lunch, a movie—did you know they're showing *It's a Wonderful Life* all day at the theater for the next four days? And then dinner here. It was a blast."

"It was indeed." Alice smiled while Hayley rolled her eyes at Emma.

Nick arrived at the table and placed two old-fashioned glasses down, sliding one over to Emma.

"Here are your drinks," Nick added. "Do you think I can convince you to play a little bit tonight, Noah?"

"Oh, I don't know, Nick," Noah hedged. He looked toward the stage and saw the trio getting ready for their next set. "It looks like you have all the entertainment you need."

"It's the same guys from the other night, but their sax player finally made it. I'm sure they wouldn't mind if you sat in for a bit."

"You played here?" Clay asked.

Noah sat back in the booth quietly and said nothing, but Emma jumped in.

"He sure did," she added proudly. "It was only a couple of songs, but it was great. He even played 'Christmastime,' Mom. You would have loved it."

"Oh, I would love to hear you play, Noah," Alice said hopefully.

"Don't pressure the man, Alice," Clay chided. "If he doesn't want to play anything—"

"It's okay," Noah relented as he rose from the booth, taking his drink with him. "As long as they don't mind, I'll play a few with them, Nick."

"Fantastic!" Nick said, clapping his hands together and leading Noah toward the stage.

Noah reached the stage and took the few steps up to where the trio stood, getting ready to play.

"Hey, guys." Noah nodded. "Is it okay if I sit in for a bit?"

"Rex," the bass player piped up, pointing to the saxophonist. "This is the guy I was telling you about—the piano player. He's incredible. Yeah, man, you can sit in with us."

Noah saw Rex looking him over skeptically, wondering if Noah had what it took to play with them.

"You know jazz standards?" Rex quizzed. "I like to riff on the classics, so I hope you can keep up."

"Don't worry about me," Noah said confidently. "I think I can stay with you."

"Dude, you don't recognize him?" the drummer added as he rubbed his beard. "He's Noah Healy. He plays with Diagnosis. I looked you up, man, after you played with us. You've got some great stuff. I'm sorry I didn't recognize you."

"It's probably better you didn't." Noah laughed. "But thanks."

"So he plays in an old rock band, big fucking deal," Rex tossed in. "Don't F this up for us. We've got a pretty good gig here."

"I promise," Noah said, crossing his heart.

"We're starting with Coltrane," Rex said seriously. "'In a Sentimental Mood.' Count us off, Ron," Rex indicated to the drummer.

It was a song Noah hadn't played in many years, but he knew well. So he took over the Duke Ellington part and made it his own, drawing out the keyboard play perfectly to match Rex's romanticism on the sax. When it hit the piano solo, Noah embodied the spirit of Duke with his sublime play on the keys. The music carried him away in a manner that no rock song had done in many years.

When he finished playing, he saw the smiles from Ron and Art, the bassist, and a look of complete surprise from Rex as the audience applauded. They followed it up with a more upbeat song, "Come Rain or Come Shine," which let Noah play a bit more with his talents on the solos he got to undertake. As the applause grew more robust at the end of that number, Rex turned to Noah at the keyboards.

"I'm sorry, man," Rex apologized. "The guys said you were the real deal. They were right."

"No worries." Noah smiled.

"What next?" Art whispered over to Rex. Rex turned to Noah.

"Anything you want to play?"

"Let's try this one," Noah said, pointing at the pencil-scrawled playlist he saw on top of the piano.

"I don't sing," Rex added cautiously. "We can play it instrumentally."

"I can sing," Noah added confidently.

Noah hunched over the keyboard, glancing toward the back corner to make sure he caught Emma's eyes. He smiled in her direction and then started to play, his fingers striking each key perfectly. He kept looking at Emma as he saw the recognition come to her face, and she beamed.

Noah didn't recall ever singing "Over the Rainbow" either to himself or anyone else, but the words came to him as if they were there all the time, just waiting for him to draw them out. There were few interludes that he allowed for solo piano play and other moments for the rest of the quartet, but his playing took over front and center. As Noah sang each verse, he made sure to open his eyes and look at Emma. Even through the lighting shining on him transitioning to the dimness of the corner, he could see Emma with her hands locked under her chin, mouthing the lyrics along with him.

Whistling and clapping filled the pub, even with the place only half-filled, when Noah was done. He gave a slow nod of his head and took a sip of his scotch before turning things back over to Rex. Noah sat in for a couple of more tunes, following the lead of the rest of the band before he noticed Emma pointing at her watch, letting him know it was nearing time for her to get to work.

"I can do one more, guys," Noah said. "How about a Christmas tune before I'm done?"

Rex nodded in agreement, and the band consulted briefly on which one to perform before choosing what was best. Noah started playing "The Christmas Song" immediately, with the other band members joining in as he went along. His choice delighted the crowd, particularly Emma and her parents. Noah channeled his inner Nat King Cole, considering this one his favorite version, and did his best to honor the jazz pianist as he played until he finished the short holiday number.

Applause rose once again as Rex announced they were taking a break and thanked Noah for sitting in with them.

"Dude, you can jam with us any time you want," Rex said, shaking hands with Noah.

"Thanks," Noah answered. "You guys are good. It was a pleasure."

Noah made his way back to the corner booth, acknowledging people along the way who complimented him on his performance.

"Noah, that was fantastic," Alice gushed when he arrived back at the table. "What a wonderful treat. I never knew you had such a lovely voice. You should sing more."

"Never mind the singing," Clay added. "You were tearing it up on the piano. Ellington would have been proud of your 'In a Sentimental Mood.' Fine work, Noah."

"Thank you both. That means a lot to me," Noah said humbly. Noah had placed his hand in his lap and felt Emma sneak over and grab it.

"Yes, very nice," Hayley said. "No offense, but my food is finished, and I can't stand sitting here drinking soda anymore. Can we go home, please?"

"I have to get going to work anyway," Emma announced. Noah stood up, polishing off his scotch so that Emma could step out as well. "I'll see you all in the morning."

"Have a good night, honey," Clay added while he shook Noah's hand. "Noah, will we get to see you again? I promise not to put you to work if we do."

"I'm sure you'll see me again," Noah promised.

Noah approached the bar where Nick stood, holding court with a few of the regulars. Noah pulled money out of his wallet to hand to Nick, who abruptly refused.

"No way," Nick said, waving it off. "You come in here and play like that, and you will always get drinks on the house. That much I can promise you. So make sure he sticks around, Emma."

Emma laughed uncomfortably before they left the pub, and the two walked silently for a bit before they neared the hotel, the only sound of their footsteps crunching the rock salt beneath their feet.

When they reached the hotel's front door, Emma turned to Noah and looked into his face.

"I had such a wonderful day with you, from start to finish," Emma gushed. "I don't want it to end. I feel like Cinderella with midnight approaching."

"I know you have to go to work, but I'll see you in the morning. I promise," Noah said as he took Emma's hands in his.

"It's… it's not just that, Noah," Emma said. "Eventually, your band will have everything fixed, and you'll have to go. Then who knows when—or if—I'll see you again."

"Why would you say that?"

"Because it's true," Emma admitted. "You have a whole other life outside of here, Noah. You'll step away from here and be back out on the road. You don't know when you'll be back this way again. Goodness knows, Emerald Lake isn't going to be on your next tour schedule."

"Let's not think about that right now," Noah implored. "We still have a few more days together, including Christmas. We don't have any shows planned until after the new year, and I sure don't want to spend Christmas in my apartment alone eating takeout Chinese, even if we could get out of here. I would much rather spend it here, with you."

"I would love that," Emma added with elation, giving Noah a big hug.

Noah led Emma inside the hotel as they both moved toward the front desk. Emma was surprised to see Marianne standing there, smiling.

"Hey, you're back!" Emma said happily.

"Finally," Marianne answered. "Thank goodness Gary got home to help plow everything out and get the electric back on. I was getting worried. Bernadette was less than thrilled as well. And who do we have here?" Marianne turned her eyes to Noah.

"Oh, Noah Healy, this is Marianne Bailey. Marianne typically works the afternoon/evening shift here.

Noah is… an old family friend in the area for a few days," Emma said cautiously.

"Nice to meet you, Noah." Marianne smiled.

"Are you related to George Bailey at the eyeglass shop?" Noah asked.

Marianne looked on with surprise.

"I am," she answered. "He's my father. Did he sell you a pair of glasses?"

"No, but I've heard about him." Noah smiled, looking at Emma.

"We ran into Mrs. Travers this morning," Emma added.

"Oh." Marianne laughed. "I'll let you in on a bit of a secret. My dad has been sweet on Mrs. Travers for years. He constantly fusses with her glasses to make sure she comes back and needs something adjusted just so he can see her. It's kind of cute."

"Well, I should let you get to work," Noah said, stretching. "It's nice to meet you, Marianne."

"I'll walk you to the elevator," Emma insisted, tagging along with Noah around the corner to the elevator bank.

"Thank you again," Emma said sweetly. Noah wrapped his arms around her, kissing her deeply.

"Are you sure I can't convince you to come upstairs with me? It's going to be kind of lonely after being with you all day."

"Hmmm, it's tempting, but I better not. You'll just have to dream about me." Emma smiled.

"No problem there," Noah replied as the elevator door opened. He stepped inside and pressed the three button to head up to his room.

"See you in the morning?" he asked as the door began to close.

"You better!" Emma yelled to him as the door shut.

****

Emma waltzed back to the front desk, humming "Over the Rainbow" once again and smiling. It wasn't until she saw Marianne following each step she took with her eyes that she stopped.

"What?" Emma asked as she stored her purse in the back office.

"You're kidding me, right?" Marianne said.

Emma shrugged at Marianne, still oblivious to what she was referring to.

"You come in here on the arm of some handsome man I've never seen around here. You walk him to the elevator, smooching noises echo through the lobby, and then you come back grinning and humming. And you're wearing a skirt, for crying out loud! You owe me more of an explanation than he's an old family friend."

"He is an old friend," Emma defended. "He was a college roommate of Paul's."

"He's that Noah?" Marianne exclaimed. "I remember him. He didn't look that way when he was eighteen, for sure. He and Paul would come down to the lake and flirt with me and—"

"Erin Miley, I know, I know," Emma said with envy.

"Yes! They were corny. You always had a crush on him, didn't you? I can see nothing has changed."

"Well, some things have changed," Emma said slyly.

"Emma Louise Birch, what have you done?" Marianne said in mock shock. "If I didn't have to get home to Gary and the kids, I would want every saucy detail. But geez, I'm gone for two days, and look at you! So be prepared to text me tonight. I need to know more about this."

"I will. I promise." Emma laughed as she put the Christmas music on a bit louder. "Anything I need to know about?"

"Nah, we had a few check-ins this afternoon, but I don't think anyone is due to come in still today," Marianne answered as she gathered her belongings. "It should be a quiet night for you."

"Good," Emma said as she pinned on her name tag and donned her Santa hat. "I'm pooped. Is there anything in the fridge? I didn't get to grab anything before I left the house."

"Seems to me you grabbed something." Marianne cackled. "I think there are a couple of things in the freezer. If I remember, I'll bring some of the chicken pot pie I made down tomorrow and leave some here for you. Have a good night, Em."

Emma watched as Marianne strolled out into the night. She returned to the back office, rummaging through the refrigerator and freezer until she found a frozen lasagna she could throw in the microwave. Even with Perry Como singing "Jingle Bells" on the speakers, Emma couldn't shake "Over the Rainbow" from her head. She danced her way across the lobby floor, her skirt flowing lightly as she moved until she reached the Christmas tree. She plucked a couple of plastic ornaments that had fallen on the floor and placed them gingerly back on their appropriate branches before straightening the strands of the garland so the tree looked perfect.

Marianne wasn't joking when she said it would be a quiet night. Outside of the beep of the microwave when her less-than-satisfying lasagna was done and the array of Christmas tunes playing, silence reigned over the front desk area for most of the night. However, Emma did spend some time texting with Marianne, letting her know about her day with Noah while leaving out some of the sexier details involved.

It was about three in the morning when Emma was polishing the front counter when she heard the sound of the elevator coming down. The usual sound of the door sliding open occurred, and Emma listened to a soft patter on the floor approach. She turned to see Noah standing there, barefoot, wearing just a T-shirt and a pair of red plaid sleep pants.

"What are you doing awake?" Emma asked as Noah neared her.

"I did sleep for a little bit, and I did dream about you," he told her. "But I woke up and wanted to see the real thing."

Noah pulled Emma close and started to lightly kiss her neck, adding soft nibbles along the way.

"Come upstairs with me," Noah whispered.

"Noah, I can't," Emma insisted. "I'm working. Someone has to stay down here."

"There's no one around. It's three a.m. No one will know," Noah tempted. Instead, Noah kissed under Emma's chin, moving around to the other side of her neck and close to her ear, causing her to giggle.

"You need to control yourself," she scolded as she walked back behind the front desk counter.

"It's too late for that," Noah told her as he followed Emma behind the counter. He peeked into the back office to check around and then popped back out, taking Emma by the hand and pulling her into the back room.

Noah returned to his kissing, slowly working on wearing down Emma's armor. Emma let Noah's hands roam everywhere as she turned flush. Noah pushed Emma up against the near wall, kissing her with more passion now as his hands moved down her body. Emma returned the caresses, her hands gripping Noah's back to hold him tightly.

Noah's hand found the hem of Emma's skirt and steadily began to lift it until his hand reached the top of her left thigh.

"See the advantages of wearing a skirt," Noah growled as his fingers rubbed the front of her thin panties, causing her to gasp loudly.

All Emma could do was nod in agreement as her hand went from trying to prevent Noah's wrist from moving higher to holding his hand in place as he caressed her. Finally, two of Noah's fingers slipped inside her as Emma ground her pelvis against Noah's hand, holding on to him tightly as she moaned into his shoulder to muffle the noise.

Noah picked Emma up by the waist as she wrapped her legs around him. He moved from the wall over to a small table just inside the room, pushing the stacks of paper and office material onto the floor in a frenzy.

Emma's hands went for the waist of Noah's pants, pushing them down so that she could get at him before Noah stopped her.

"I didn't bring anything down with me," Noah said between deep breaths.

"What?" Emma said, running her hand through her hair before she laid her head against the wall behind her. "Sorry, I don't have any pockets this time."

"I thought I'd convince you to come upstairs with me," Noah lamented. "I'm sorry."

"It's okay," Emma said, catching her breath. "It's probably for the best."

Emma looked at Noah's face and saw the smile creep across his face as he grabbed Emma's hips and pulled her toward the edge of the table. His hands quickly snaked up her legs to pull down her damp panties before she had much time to protest. Noah lifted Emma's skirt slowly before burying his head between her thighs, drawing a low moan from Emma.

Without thought, Emma's hands went to Noah's hair, running through it as he kissed, licked, and nibbled at her. Her gasping and panting drowned out the sound of the Christmas music echoing through the lobby. Then, when Noah's tongue flicked across the tip of her clitoris, Emma groaned.

"Oh, God, Noah," Emma let out.

Emma thought she heard the faint sound of footsteps on the tile floor in the lobby, but the intense passion she felt in her body filled her ears as well. It wasn't until she heard the distinct sound of someone clearing their throat in the lobby that she and Noah froze in place.

"Hello?" she heard a woman's voice speak.

"Yes?" Emma's voice cracked at a high pitch, still not moving.

"I'm sorry, I know it's late," the woman said. "I was wondering if I could get a couple of bottles of soda from the pantry."

"Sure, go right ahead," Emma said, still too scared to move. She glanced down at Noah, who did all he could to keep from laughing. She saw that grin on his face again, and he moved his face forward once again, sliding his tongue up and down on her. Emma gasped again, this time gripping Noah's hair in her fingers tightly as he worked on her.

"Is everything okay?" the woman's voice asked with concern.

"Yes, I'm fine, thanks," Emma said shakily. "Do you need anything else?" Noah's tongue dipped deeper into her and then swirled over her clit. Emma brought her right hand up to cover her mouth and capture her groan as she closed her eyes.

"I think that's it," the woman said in a confused tone. "Do I need to pay for these?"

"Just... just tell me your room number, and I'll charge your room," Emma rushed out, feeling her thighs start to shake.

"Okay, it's 201."

"Got it," Emma said, straining to hold on. "Have a good night."

Footsteps trailed away, and Emma heard the elevator just as her orgasm hit, leaving her quivering and holding Noah in place.

Noah pulled away, standing up and then embracing Emma tightly as both broke out in laughter.

"You can probably cross that off your bucket list now," Noah said into Emma's ear.

"You're determined to get me fired, aren't you?" she said in mock anger, slapping Noah's shoulder.

"I would have stopped if you really wanted me to," Noah confessed. "All you had to do was ask."

"And just how was I supposed to do that?" Emma asked as she hopped off the table and picked her panties off the floor before stepping into them and straightening her skirt.

"I don't know. You didn't seem to have a problem talking to room 201." Noah laughed. "Don't forget to charge her room for those sodas, by the way."

"You're evil," Emma replied.

"Welcome to the dark side," Noah said with a sinister laugh.

Emma charged over to Noah and hugged him before giving him a kiss and looking into his face.

"I think I love you," she whispered and then quickly brought her hand up to her mouth fearfully.

Noah took a step back and looked at Emma with surprise.

"I—I don't know why I said that," Emma spoke. "It just came out. Noah, don't—"

"It's okay," Noah said, composed. He stepped close to Emma again, running his hand through her hair.

"Don't freak out, okay?" Emma rushed. "I didn't mean to say that now."

"I will freak out," Noah stated calmly, touching Emma's cheek. "Especially if you tell me you didn't mean to say it and want to take it back."

12

The incessant thumping on the door showed no signs of stopping, no matter how many pillows Noah placed over his head. So when he finally heard the scream of "Open the fucking door, Noah!" come from the hallway in the all too familiar refrain that Ray used, Noah rose and stormed to the door, flinging it open and surprising Ray and Cecil on the other side.

"I'm sorry, Noah," Cecil said sincerely. "He wouldn't listen to me."

"It's fine," Noah mumbled. "Come on in, Ray, before you piss off everyone else in the hotel."

"Where the fuck have you been for days?" Ray barked before plopping down in the chair in the room.

"Where everyone else has been," Noah said as he pulled his T-shirt on. "Here in Emerald Lake."

"Don't be a smart-ass," Ray answered. "Every time I try to get a hold of you, you aren't here. You're off gallivanting somewhere doing fuck knows what. I needed you and couldn't find you."

"You couldn't find me, or you sent Cecil, and when he didn't, you whined to Jerry about it so he would call me a hundred times? What was the problem, Ray? You couldn't find a gold toenail clipper, or there was too much mustard on your hot dog?"

Noah glanced over at Ray, who sat in stunned silence that someone would talk back to him. Noah reached for his jeans and slid into them.

"It doesn't matter what I needed you for, Noah," Ray finally answered. "The fact is, I couldn't find you, and I want to know why."

"I was out. That's all you need to know. It's not like we had anything else going on. We're stuck here, remember?"

"Actually," Cecil interrupted, "the Thruway is opened back up now. So we can head out whenever we want, I guess. Jerry said they're working on getting a sub trailer to haul our gear back to the city."

"What's the rush?" Noah asked. "We don't have any shows until after the first."

"You don't want to get out of this place?" Ray fumed. "This may as well be a black hole on the map. There is nothing here. I can't even get the shampoo I use here."

"Horror of horrors," Noah trembled.

"What the fuck has gotten into you?" Ray said, standing up to confront Noah. "You finally get your balls back? Maybe now you can write me something good to sing instead of the shit you've served up— oh, wait—you haven't even done that in five years! I don't know why we keep you around."

"Maybe because it's my fucking band, Ray." Noah snarled. "Or did you forget all about that when Jack and I plucked you out of that wedding band you were working with in college, singing Carpenter songs over and over?"

"Jack had the right idea when he left your sorry ass."

"Jack didn't leave my ass," Noah shot back. "He left because of you! You drove us into the ground, Ray. Spending every fucking penny you got as soon as it came in to the point where we had to tour three-quarters of the year to pay off debts, back taxes, and God knows what else. He was tired of being a slave to you and this. Jack was the smart one. I was stupid enough to think I could make it work by kissing your ass."

"No one is keeping you here! Finding a second-rate piano player who doesn't write songs isn't that hard in the music world, Noah. We can have you replaced in an hour, right, Cecil?"

Noah looked at Cecil, who stood by silently.

"Is all this because of that piece of ass Edgar says you've been hanging out with?" Ray spat.

"What did you say?" Noah growled.

"You finally get pussy from some groupie, and now you're whipped." Ray laughed. "Trust me, Noah, whoever she is, there is another one in the next town who looks better and fucks just as sweet. Move on."

Noah stepped toward Ray before Cecil intervened.

"Cecil, you better get him out of here before I knock his fucking teeth out," Noah warned.

"Don't worry, Cecil." Ray laughed. "He doesn't have the balls. That woman probably has them wrapped up in her purse by now. Besides, he doesn't want to damage his delicate hands."

Noah lunged toward Ray, but Cecil wrapped his arms around him and pushed him away.

Noah struggled to get at Ray as he noticed Edgar and Jordan enter the room. Edgar rushed over to help Cecil push Noah back while Jordan stood by, unsure of what to do.

"Noah, calm down," Edgar said, trying to get a grip on Noah's arms.

"I'm done with him, Eddie!" Noah shouted. "He's been dragging us down and around for years. I can't do it anymore!"

"We're done with you, Noah!" Ray yelled back. "We're all equal members in this band, remember? It's in our contract. So we can vote you out. I'm sure Jordan and Pete will back me up. It's not like you contribute anything to us anyway."

Noah heard the murmur of a small crowd filling up the hallway outside the room, but the droning on of Ray was all he could pay attention to until he heard a small voice in the room.

"Noah? What's going on?"

All eyes in the room turned to see Emma standing there, her coat draped over her arm.

Ray burst out laughing when he saw Emma standing there.

"Really, Noah? This is what you're going to piss your career away for? Look at her! She's a night clerk at a hotel in the middle of Bumfuck, New York! She's a wallflower who can brag on TikTok that she fucked a musician. Get your head together, man. You'll find a better piece of ass in the city—someone with tits and good looks, at least."

Noah saw nothing but red and yelled as loudly as he could. Pushing Cecil and Edgar aside so he could land a punch squarely on Ray's nose, drawing blood immediately. As Ray staggered, Noah grabbed him by the collar of his paisley shirt and rammed him into the closet door, splintering it as soon as Ray thudded against it. Ray slumped to the floor, the wind knocked out of him before Noah planted a couple of kicks to Ray's midsection.

"Repeat it, you son of a bitch, so I can knock your fucking teeth out," Noah shouted.

Ray turned rapidly, punching Noah below the right eye to send him reeling back, knocking the TV off the dresser and sending it to the floor.

"I said she never would have made it to the arena, never mind the backstage couch with me." Ray grinned as blood dripped down his face. "Sorry, honey, but you aren't worth the trouble. You should run along. We'll leave you some extra cash at the desk when we check out for your troubles," he added, turning toward Emma.

Noah sprang up from the floor, hitting Ray on the chin as hard as possible, so he hit the mirror on the far wall, shattering it. Noah moved over, grabbing Ray again, readying to hit him.

"Noah, don't!" Emma pled, grabbing Noah's arm to prevent him from punching again. "He's not worth it."

"You better listen to your little girl there, Noah." Ray laughed again, spitting more blood from his mouth. "You should have come knocking on my door, honey. Then at least you could tell your other lonely Facebook friends you fucked an absolute rock star and not a has-been backup."

Noah reared back to hit Ray again, sending Emma tumbling back, so she bounced off the bed and hit the floor. Noah turned to see what happened, but before moving toward Emma, the room was cleared by three police officers, including one who tackled Noah.

"Move, and I will Taser you!" the officer shouted, twisting Noah's hands behind his back so he could handcuff them.

Noah turned his head to the side to look at Emma and saw her sitting on the floor at the foot of the bed. He wriggled in his handcuffs, trying to move toward Emma as the police officer drove his knee into Noah's back.

"Alan, stop," Emma begged. "It wasn't his fault."

"I saw him throw you to the floor, Emma," Alan barked. "That's assault. Do not move!"

Noah groaned as the knee moved on him again. He watched as Emma moved closer to him, bringing her face down on the floor near his.

"Are you okay? I'm sorry," Emma said, tears forming in her eyes.

"I'm fine," Noah grunted. "Are you all right?"

Emma nodded, drawing her face closer to Noah's. He inched nearer to her again, and Emma reached her hand out to touch his head.

"I said don't move!" Alan yelled once more.

Noah felt a jolt course through his body as the Taser jabbed into his ribcage, causing him to black out before he could do anything else.

****

Noah remained groggy through most of the morning, from when they loaded him into the back of the squad car until he was booked and placed in a holding cell at the small Emerald Lake Police Department. Then, alone in the dank enclosure, Noah stretched out on the thin wooden bench and stared up at the water-stained ceiling before closing his eyes, hoping it would make the throbbing headache he had go away.

Ray had clocked him well, leaving a sizeable mouse under his right eye and a ringing in his ears. From what he overheard while lying there, Ray was on the worse side of it, insisting he be brought to the hospital to get checked out. Police were there, holding him at the emergency room while they worked on a broken nose, damaged teeth, and bruised ribs. Just the thought of Ray having black eyes and a broken nose for days to come proved enough to make Noah smile weakly.

Noah heard the outer door open and slam shut, and then heavy footsteps came in his direction. Noah pried his left eye barely open, sensitive to the light flickering above him, to spy an officer standing outside beyond the jail cell.

"You up?" the voice bellowed.

"Seems like it." Noah sighed as he swung his legs down, his head aching as he lifted it up.

The officer opened a folder, flipping the top page back and forth. Noah glanced over and could see the name tag of Embree gleaming under the light.

"Noah Healy?" Officer Embree commented.

"That's me."

"We're still trying to work everything out regarding what you'll be charged with. Mr."—Embree looked down at the sheet again—"Mr. Raymond Magnuson still hasn't decided if he is pressing charges of assault and battery against you. We haven't heard back from the Emerald Hotel either regarding the damages you caused. And then there's the situation with Ms. Birch."

"What situation with Ms. Birch?" Noah asked.

"You assaulted her," Officer Embree stated. "I witnessed it."

"I never laid a hand on her," Noah asserted.

Officer Embree flipped the paper once more.

"You pushed her across the room, where she fell and bruised her arm. I took a picture of the bruise if you would like to see it."

"That was completely accidental," Noah said. "She was trying to keep me from hitting Ray again when he struck me. You're completely twisting this around. Did she say she wanted to press charges?"

"No, not exactly," Embree answered. "But I'm—I mean, we're still investigating and speaking with her. Based on your previous record, however, there does appear to be a pattern here."

"What previous record? I've never even had a traffic ticket!"

"An incident at Oneonta back in 2010," Officer Embree read. "You and others were detained because of drunk and disorderly, underage drinking, and destruction of property."

"You've got to be kidding me with this," Noah said, exasperated. "I was twenty, in college, and with a bunch of other guys, including Paul Birch, her brother. There was no violence. We overturned some garbage cans. Those charges were dropped for community service."

"Don't even mention the name Paul Birch here," Officer Embree yelled. "The guy's a goddamn war hero who wouldn't be in the same room with you! You'll be staying away from the Birch family, especially Emma."

"Can I speak with her?"

"Not a chance," Embree scoffed.

"Okay, well, can I at least make a call so I can get a lawyer here before I see the judge?"

"It's not likely you'll get to see a judge before Christmas." Embree smirked. "Judge Aaron is away until after the holiday. So you'll be our guest until he gets back to arraign you."

"I'm still entitled to contact someone," Noah pressed. "I'd like to do that—now."

Officer Embree had the cell opened so Noah could step out and use the phone on the lone desk nearest the jail area. The policeman watched Noah closely to see the number he was dialing. Noah had no idea what phone number Emma had at the moment, but he knew who he needed to call anyway. Finally, after three rings, Jerry answered.

"Noah, what the fuck?" Jerry said into the phone.

"Jesus, Jerry, where are you?'

"I'm here at this hole-in-the-wall hospital with Ray. Eddie filled me in on what happened. Why did you have to break his nose? And a few teeth as well? He's a mess."

"Good," Noah replied. "They're holding me in jail, and they say it's until after Christmas. Assault charges and destruction of property."

"I'm already working on that," Jerry told him. "I'm talking to the hotel, and we'll just pay for the damages, and they won't press charges. So Ray won't press any charges against you as long as you don't against him. Is that cool with you?"

"Yeah, fine," Noah agreed, as much as he wanted to give Ray a hard time.

"So that should cover everything, right?" Jerry asked.

"Maybe not," Noah answered as he glanced at Alan Embree. "They're talking about charges against me for hitting Twig—I mean, Emma."

"The front desk girl? Why would they do that? Did you hit her?" Jerry asked in a hushed tone.

"Of course not!" Noah protested loudly, drawing a stern look from Embree. "No, but I think there are extenuating circumstances around it that I can't get into over the phone."

"All right, let me see what I can find out and do on my end. It might take me a little bit to get everything sorted out, so just hang tight. As soon as

Ray is settled here, I'll head over there. You need anything else?"

"I don't think so," Noah added. "Thanks, Jerry."

Noah hung up the phone and looked at Officer Embree, who simply pointed back to the jail cell so Noah would get back in.

Noah shuffled back into the jail and heard the lock shut behind him. He sat on the wooden bench, shoulders slumped, rubbing his grizzled face in his hands.

"How long have you known Emma Birch?" Officer Embree asked.

Noah remained silent, not even acknowledging the question.

"Did you hear me?" Embree emphasized.

"I heard you," Noah answered. "I don't see how it's any of your business."

"It is my business when I'm conducting an investigation. Now, how long have you known Emma Birch?"

"About twelve years, I guess," Noah relented. "Her brother and I were college roommates. So I've known the family for a long time."

"Funny, I've never seen you around here, and I've been in Emerald Lake for about five years. You can't be very close," Embree added.

"I don't make it up this way much," Noah said, giving a narrowing glare to Embree. "My work has me going all over the place."

"Right, the rock musician." Embree laughed. He looked down at his folder again. "Diagnosis. I can't say I've ever heard of you."

"I'll make sure to get you a signed CD," Noah grumbled.

"Is that some kind of a bribe?" Embree barked.

"Look, I don't know how many cop movies or TV shows you have watched that have made you like this, but you must have something better to do than this tough guy, Brain Denehy in *First Blood* act."

Noah lay back on the bench and stared up at the ceiling when he heard the cell door slide open again. Embree stood over Noah, staring down at him.

"You think this is all a joke, don't you?" Embree said, gritting his teeth. Beads of sweat formed just under the crewcut Embree wore.

"I don't think the law is a joke," Noah answered. "You, on the other hand, I am having thoughts about."

"You weren't so funny when I was using the Taser on you," Embree grunted, gripping the Taser on his holster.

"What's your relationship with Emma Birch?" Embree asked, bringing his face closer to Noah's.

"None of your fucking business," Noah retaliated. "That's what this is all about, isn't it? I heard about your slight obsession with her, asking her out all the time and getting rejected. That must suck for you."

Embree reached down and put his hand around Noah's throat and started to squeeze.

"Accidents happen all the time in jail cells," Embree said quietly. "I'd be careful what you say."

"And if I were you, I'd be careful what you do," Noah croaked out, his face getting red. "Those cameras are pointed right at you if you want to give a wave."

Embree's eyes shot up and glanced at the cameras in the corners pointed inside the jail cell before he let go of Noah. Noah gasped for air before moving away from Embree.

The officer walked out of the cell and closed the door.

"Get comfortable, asshole." Embree smiled. "You're in for a long stay."

****

Emma grew restless waiting in the emergency room at the hospital just outside of Emerald Lake. She didn't want to get checked out, but Alan Embree insisted she get examined by EMTs and sent off, even though all she had was a small bruise on her arm from the fall. When her father strolled into the ER looking for her, it made the situation even worse.

"Emma, what's going on? Are you okay?" Clay asked with concern.

"I'm fine, Dad," Emma insisted. "I just got a bruise on my arm. It's no big deal."

"What happened?"

"Noah got into a pretty nasty fight with one of the band members. Punches were thrown, stuff broke, and I tried to get in the middle of it to stop him and got pushed. Then all hell broke loose when the police showed up."

"Alan called me to tell me you were here," Clay replied.

"Don't listen to everything Alan has to say, Dad. He's making it seem much worse than it is. Besides that, he used his Taser on Noah for no real reason."

"He said you were in danger."

"I was trying to talk to Noah to see what happened. I was never in danger. Noah—Noah wouldn't hurt me. Alan spent most of the time trying to convince me to press assault charges against Noah."

"What?" Clay said in shock.

"I didn't do it, and I'm not going to, Dad. Don't worry. He didn't do anything except try to defend me. The whole thing is a big mess. I just hope Noah is okay," Emma answered.

"They're holding him at the Emerald Lake Police Station," Clay told her. "Alan let me know he was there. They can't arraign him until Judge Aaron is around, and that might not be for days."

"Where's Judge Aaron?' Emma asked. "Noah can't just sit in jail for days on end."

"If I know Vince Aaron, he's just home for Christmas with the grandkids. So he probably doesn't know anything about any of this yet." Clay walked over and gave Emma a hug. "I'm just glad you're okay," Clay said with an extra squeeze.

"Dad, do you think you could go check on Noah? I'm worried about him having to sit in there."

"Let me make some phone calls," Clay assured her. "I'll see what I can find out."

"Thanks," she answered, relieved.

Emma watched her father leave, and the ER doctor entered her area almost immediately after.

"How are you feeling?" the doctor asked, looking over Emma's bruise.

"I feel fine," Emma insisted. "I think I could just go. There's nothing wrong."

"The police report says you were assaulted, Ms. Birch. If there's anything you want to tell me…" the female doctor asked before her voice trailed off.

"The report is wrong," Emma stated forcefully. "I was pushed, accidentally. I landed on the floor and bruised my arm. I don't need to be here."

A light knock outside the curtain occurred before it pulled slightly. Emma saw a short man, stocky, wearing a wrinkled suit, standing before her.

"Are you Emma Birch?" the man questioned, scratching his scraggly beard.

"Yes, I am," Emma answered.

"Just the person I'm looking for." The man smiled, moving forward.

"Sir, I'm in the middle of business here," the doctor interrupted. "Can this wait a few minutes?"

"It sounded like the young lady said she was done here if I overheard her correctly. Is that right, Ms. Birch?"

Emma nodded, curious as to who the man was and what he wanted.

The doctor sighed and shrugged.

"I'll have a nurse come by in a bit with your discharge papers," the doctor told Emma before exiting the area.

Emma's full attention now turned to the man, who reached into his inner suit jacket pocket and pulled out a business card.

"I'm Jerry Martin, manager of the band Diagnosis," he said formally. "I take it you know a few people in the group, based on today's activity."

"I really only know Noah," Emma said, running her thumb and index finger over the business card.

"Right, Noah," Jerry said, scratching his beard again. "Here's the thing, Ms. Birch—I mean, Emma, if I can call you that?'

Emma nodded and listened.

"Noah's stuck in jail because the police said you're pressing assault charges," Jerry began.

"I never said that to anyone!" Emma said with a raised voice before realizing others could hear her.

"The police are the ones pushing that, not me. I wasn't assaulted."

"Yes, I heard you say that to the doctor and now again to me, which is great," Jerry answered. "Are you willing to sign something that says that? It will help us to get things cleared up faster, and I'll be more than happy to, um, compensate you for any of the troubles all this has caused you, including any bills you get for this ER visit."

"I'm not looking to get any money out of this, Mr. Martin," Emma replied. "I just want to know that Noah is okay."

"Perfect." Jerry grinned. "I spoke with him a bit ago. He's said he is doing okay and was concerned about you as well. I'm sure he'll be glad to hear that you're fine and aren't pressing charges."

"Did—did he think I was going to press charges against him?" Emma asked with concern.

"Oh, I don't think so, but you never know how these things are going to go, Ms. Birch," Jerry said as he pulled out his cell phone. "People find out you're in the music business and suddenly want to sue you or get their names in the news. It's my job to make sure the band is protected, is all."

Clay walked back into Emma's area in the ER, and Emma saw the surprise on her father's face when he saw Jerry in there.

"Who is this?" Clay questioned.

"I'm Jerry Martin, sir," Jerry said, offering his hand to Clay. As they shook, Jerry grinned.

"Wow, strong hands." Jerry laughed. "I'm the manager of Diagnosis."

"Is that something with the hospital here?" Clay asked, causing Jerry to laugh before realizing Clay was serious.

"No, Dad," Emma explained. "It's Noah's band. Mr. Martin here was just checking on me."

"Well, I do have some good news," Clay said, turning his attention solely to Emma. "I talked to Vince Aaron. He's going down to the station so they can have a hearing tonight and get this over with. He told me he'd talk to the attorney to see what's going on."

"Attorney, huh?" Jerry added, typing into his phone. "I guess I better get over there too. Thank you for your honesty, Ms. Birch. Like I said, I'm sure we can help you out. We'll talk again. Nice meeting you, Mr. Birch."

Jerry shuffled away from Emma and her father, leaving them confused.

"What was that all about?" Clay asked.

"He wanted to make sure I was okay and not pressing charges against Noah. He said they would pay me and take care of the hospital bill."

"Pay you for what? Doing the right thing?" Clay said.

"I don't know, Dad. It's not important. How is Noah?"

"That I couldn't get any answers about," Clay added regretfully. "Sorry, honey. They wouldn't tell me anything. Chief Larsen wasn't in for me to talk with."

"It's okay." Emma sighed. "I just want to get out of here and down to the station to make sure he's okay."

The nurse walked in with Emma's discharge papers, and she rushed through signing them to leave with her father. They stepped out into the dreary late afternoon weather. A heavy cloud cover hung in the air as a few stray flakes of snow began to fall.

Emma climbed into the passenger side of her father's truck and watched as flakes clung to the windshield and window. Then, finally, her father pulled out, leaving the parking lot behind and heading back toward Emerald Lake.

"I'm sure he's fine, honey," Clay tried to assure.

"I sure hope so," she whispered, staring out the window.

13

Hours went by with Noah alone in his cell, wondering what was going on. The worry wasn't for Ray, the band, or how much it might cost to take care of the damages the fight caused. Instead, Noah's most significant concern was regarding Emma. The confusing interrogation he had with Officer Embree left him wondering if Emma had misinterpreted what happened somehow or was injured worse than he had thought. The more time he had to consider it, the worse things became in Noah's brain.

With no watch, no phone, and no windows in the cell, Noah had no idea what time it was or how long he had been in jail. It wasn't until another officer, not Embree, came in and unlocked the door.

"Get up," the policeman commanded to Noah.

Noah rose from the bench, feeling aches in his muscles from being there and the fight, and he shuffled toward the officer. The policeman made a spinning motion with his finger before Noah reached him, indicating he should turn around. Instead, Noah heard the distinct click of the handcuffs before they were placed around his wrists.

"I guess I'm not leaving yet," Noah said sarcastically.

"Not likely," the gruff cop answered before leading Noah out the door and down a hallway until they reached the end. The officer opened the door labeled "Courtroom," and Noah entered, the lighting so much brighter than what he had been exposed to that he squinted immediately. Once his vision adjusted to the light, he spotted Jerry toward the back of the courtroom talking with a tall man in a suit. He scanned the gallery and spotted Pete and Eddie sitting there as well.

Officer Embree was perched in the front row, behind the prosecution desk, scowling as he spotted Noah. As Noah sat at his assigned desk and was uncuffed, he looked around again, this time seeing no signs of Emma anywhere. His heart sank slightly as he worried about what the proceedings might hold.

The back door swung open to the courtroom, and Noah spun around to look, only to see Greg Evans, the band's attorney, enter and start talking with Jerry and the other man. Noah looked on, surprised Greg had actually come up from New York City to take care of this himself. He saw Greg and Jerry go from serious to smiling in a matter of seconds before both started to move toward him. Jerry ducked into the first row with Pete and Edgar before Greg came around and sat with Noah.

"Everything good?" Greg asked Noah, looking him over.

"You tell me, Greg," Noah asked warily.

"I think we've got everything ironed out," Greg said confidently. "You should be out of here in a little bit. I'm sorry you had to sit around so long. It took me a lot longer to get here than I thought it would."

Noah turned back to face Jerry.

"Jerry, how's—" Before Noah could even get the words out, Jerry interrupted him.

"The Birch girl is fine," Jerry said with a nod. "She just has a couple of bruises. She's not blaming us for anything, and I told her we would take care of her."

"What does that mean?" Noah asked.

Before Jerry could answer, the courtroom door opened once more, with Emma and Clay entering. Emma locked eyes with Noah and moved toward where he was seated, with Noah rising to go and greet her. In a flash, Officer Embree stepped in front of the gate leading to the attorneys' desks to block Emma from it while the other officer grabbed hold of Noah.

"You need to sit, now, or you will be cuffed and removed," the officer commanded, forcing Noah back into his chair.

"Noah, are you okay?" Emma asked, trying to get past Embree, but he held her back.

"You can't go in there, Emma," Embree said, trying to embrace Emma.

"Take your hands off her!" Noah yelled and tried to rise from his chair before he was pushed back down. Embree just smirked at Noah, and Clay came over and took hold of Emma to guide her to one of the seats in the gallery.

Shortly after the skirmish, the court bailiff entered, ordering all to rise before Judge Aaron joined. Noah rose from his chair, the policeman still standing close by, as he watched the judge come in and sit at the bench.

Noah looked at the judge, an older man with salt-and-pepper hair and a well-trimmed beard to match.

"Well, I certainly wasn't expecting to have to do this today," Judge Aaron began, "but let's get this over with so we can all get on with our holiday plans."

The judge scanned the docket paperwork, glancing up occasionally to look at Noah and then at Officer Embree.

"Mr. Garcia, you're representing the people on this?" Judge Aaron asked.

"I am, Your Honor," Mr. Garcia said as he rose. "May counsel approach?"

Judge Aaron waved his hand forward as Mr. Garcia and Greg approached the bench. Noah looked on as they passed paperwork back and forth to the judge, whispering. Noah glanced back at Emma and saw the frightened look she had on her face.

"Okay, step back," Judge Aaron spoke.

"It seems we have a lot of conflicting information here regarding what occurred during the fight, along with some disturbing things afterward," the judge said, looking toward Officer Embree. "Under normal circumstances, I would refer this for trial sometime after the New Year, but apparently both sides have come to some kind of plea agreement?"

Noah flashed a look of confusion at Greg, who just nodded toward him without saying a word.

Mr. Garcia rose again and began talking about the agreement.

"Yes, Your Honor. The Emerald Lake Hotel has agreed to drop all charges and receive restitution for the damages caused to the room. Mr. Magnuson, Mr. Healy's bandmate, has also decided not to press assault charges against the defendant."

"So that leaves just the assault charges for what happened to Ms. Birch?" Judge Aaron noted on his paperwork.

"I never filed or wanted to press charges, Judge," Emma yelled as she rose. Clay did his best to get her to sit back down.

"Not the time or place, Emma," Judge Aaron noted. "I can see that you didn't. It was something that Officer Embree tried to push through, however. Alan, I can see Chief Larsen, and I will have a few discussions regarding you real soon. I don't know what was going through your head, boy, but you may want to see about getting a lawyer for yourself if Mr. Healy is so inclined to press charges against you."

"In any case, Your Honor," Mr. Garcia went on, "we have settled that matter as well. Accordingly, the prosecution requests the dismissal of those charges against Mr. Healy. As you can see in the paperwork, the only stipulation is the no-contact order for forty-eight hours."

"Yes, I see that here," Judge Aaron said as he looked over everything.

"Mr. Evans, is this agreement amenable to the defense?"

Greg went to rise from his chair before Noah stopped him.

"Greg, what's going on? What's the no-contact order about?" Noah whispered.

"Noah, not now," Greg insisted. "We can close this all and be done with it. Let me do my job."

Greg stood and looked at Judge Aaron. "We are aware of the terms, Your Honor, and accept them."

"Perfect." Judge Aaron smiled. He began writing on the paper in front of him. "Mr. Healy, please stand."

Noah got to his feet, still unsure of what was going on.

"All charges against the defendant are dismissed according to the plea agreement. As ordered, there is a forty-eight-hour no-contact order. Mr. Healy, you are not permitted to return to the Emerald Lake Hotel or have contact with any of the employees on-site or off, including Ms. Birch, until after the hours of the order have expired. No physical contact, no phone calls, no electronic contact at all, or the terms of the agreement are violated, and a warrant will be issued for your arrest."

"What?" Noah exclaimed. "No, that's not—"

Greg interrupted and pushed Noah back down into his seat.

"You need to stay quiet," Greg admonished. "You blow this deal, and they'll hold you in this town for who knows how long. You have a chance to walk away free and have a civil lawsuit against Dirty Harry over there."

Jerry leaned forward to add his two cents to the conversation.

"It doesn't matter, Noah. We're leaving town right after the hearing anyway. We got a gig in the city for Christmas."

"Why didn't you guys tell me any of this?" Noah argued. "I never would have gone along with this. And what do you mean we're leaving town right away? I thought we didn't have anything until after January first?"

"We didn't tell you because you would have given me grief like this," Greg added.

"Are we good to go, Mr. Evans?" Judge Aaron interjected. "I'd like to get home to have dessert with my grandkids. If there's a problem, I can reject the agreement and set a trial date. Your choice, Mr. Healy. But I need an answer now."

Noah stood, looking back and forth between Greg, Jerry, and Emma. Then, realizing he had little choice, he nodded to Greg. As soon as he did, he looked back at Emma and saw her sit down in her chair, holding her head in her hands.

"We're all good, Your Honor," Greg replied.

"Excellent," the judge exclaimed before pounding his gavel to adjourn the hearing.

Judge Aaron left the bench as Jerry, Pete, and Eddie joined Noah at the desk.

"Nice job, counselor," Eddie said, shaking Greg's hand.

Noah's gaze stayed on Emma. Clay had put an arm around her as Embree approached them. Noah heard voices raised before Emma yelled, "Get out of my face, Alan. This is all because of you!"

Noah began to move toward Emma to help her before Jerry stepped in front of him.

"Don't do that, Noah," Jerry warned. "That guy will take great pleasure in getting to arrest you again. So just let it be."

Noah looked on as Clay corralled Emma and brought her out of the courtroom and away from anyone.

"We already packed out your room at the hotel," Jerry advised. "You just have to collect your stuff from the police desk, and we can get you out of here. We're staying at the Plaza Hotel in the city tonight! Can you believe it?"

"How did you manage that?" Noah asked in wonder.

"I didn't have to do anything," Jerry said proudly. "I was sitting around trying to straighten this mess out when I got a call from Foo Fighter management. They are playing a Christmas show at the Garden, and their opening act canceled on them."

"Who was the opening act?" Noah asked glumly.

"Venereal Pus," Jerry answered.

"Those guys are still around?" Edgar added.

"Yeah. Foo Fighters wanted a 2010-era band to open, and they went with us," Jerry said proudly.

"You mean we were the only ones available," Pete told him.

"Whatever the reason is, we got the gig," Jerry told the band. "They are paying us a shitload of money, trucking our gear there, putting us up at the hotel, you name it. Do you guys realize what this exposure could do for us? We could get right back on the map, so we get bigger venues, bigger paydays, more considerable royalties. We all win from this. You guys should be kissing my feet right now."

"Sounds great," Noah said, emotionless.

"Okay, so let's go get you out of here and then get Ray from the hospital so we can get on the road and put this nightmare behind us."

"Good luck, guys," Greg said, putting his coat on. "Jerry, I'll send you my bill."

Greg left the courtroom, followed by Jerry, Pete, Eddie, and lastly, Noah. When he stepped out into the hallway to look for Emma, she was nowhere to be found.

Eddie patted Noah on the back to get his attention.

"C'mon, man. You have to let it go, at least for now. Wait a few days, and then you can see if you can come back. She may not even want you to come back."

"Why the fuck would you say that?" Noah barked, shrugging Eddie's hand from his shoulder.

"Take it easy, Noah," Eddie responded. "I'm on your side here. All I'm saying is you might feel differently once we're away from here."

"Not likely," Noah added softly as he walked toward the front desk to collect his belongings.

14

Emma returned home and went straight to her room. She spent most of the late afternoon and evening trying to decipher what happened in such a short amount of time. Everything had gone so well and then came crashing down in just a few minutes. Now Noah was gone, and she could not have any contact with him to see how he was or what might happen next. She didn't even know where he was headed after the band was ordered to leave the hotel.

Emma crashed on her bed, working through a fitful sleep until a knock on the door roused her. Hayley walked in and sat on the edge of Emma's bed, touching her leg.

"Em, you awake?" Hayley asked gently.

"I'm up," she sniffled, turning to look at her sister.

"Do you want some dinner? I made macaroni and cheese, a salad, and some biscuits. They aren't as good as yours, but Mom and Dad seemed to like them."

"I'm not hungry. Thanks," Emma answered.

"Is there anything I can do to help you?"

"I don't think so," Emma replied. She felt movement on the bed and found Hayley lying next to her and wrapping her arms around her.

"Perhaps a Hayley hug will help," Hayley said with a smile. "I used to give them to you all the time when I was little."

Emma sniffled again but giggled a bit as Hayley embraced her.

"You were so funny with hugs. You only gave them on special occasions. Paul always said it was his favorite birthday present."

"Well, it is a special occasion," Hayley added. "If I make it extra special, can this count for Christmas, too?"

"Sure," Emma replied. She rolled over to face her sister and smiled at her through her tears. "Thanks, Hayley."

"You're my sister. It's what I'm supposed to do," she said proudly.

The two hugged tightly and then lay together, staring up at the ceiling fan, holding hands.

"Are we going to make cookies tomorrow?" Hayley asked. "It's tradition, you know."

"We will, as long as I'm not too tired from work tonight."

"You're going to work tonight? After everything that happened today?" Hayley sat up and looked down at Emma.

"I have to work," Emma told her. "I need something to keep my mind off... all that."

"Going to the place where it all happened may not be the best answer to that issue, Emma. With all the trauma and everything, maybe you should just call in sick."

"No, I can do it," Emma resolved. "As a matter of fact, I'm going to go shower and get changed now."

Emma sprang off the bed before she had a chance to change her mind and crawl back under the covers. Instead, she went right to the bathroom to turn the shower on, getting it steamy hot before she climbed in to rinse off the day. When the hot water hit the minor bruises on her arm, it hurt more than Emma expected it to and winced a little but quickly pushed it out of her mind. She shut her eyes tightly as she shampooed her hair, and visions of Noah's hands running through her hair as they made love stuck with her the entire time.

After showering, she padded down to her room to dress for work, getting her cream-colored blouse and black slacks to wear before she went downstairs. She heard the Christmas music playing loudly and found her parents and Hayley gathered in the dining room, wrapping presents.

"Hey, you're up," Clay noted as he crinkled some wrapping paper over the box he was working on.

"Dad is doing presents?" Emma said with shock. "I thought you only used gift bags in protest of wrapping paper."

"Well, your mother insisted I try to get fancy this year. What do you think of this one?"

Clay held up a gift he had wrapped in white paper decorated with Christmas trees. Massive amounts of the tape showed all over, the cuts were uneven, and the corners left sharp angles where excess paper stayed.

"Did you use scissors?" Emma asked skeptically.

"Hey, I think it looks fine," Clay defended.

"Maybe you need to stick to gift bags, Dad." Hayley laughed as she munched on red and green M&M's.

"Or you could make us some more hot cocoa, Clay," Alice asked, holding up her empty mug.

"I can take a hint," Clay said, grabbing the mug and trudging off to the kitchen. Emma laughed as she followed her father, walking to the pot on the stove to scoop out some of the still warm macaroni and cheese into a Christmas bowl. She sat at the table and began to eat slowly, and Clay sat across from her as he waited for the tea kettle to whistle.

"I'm glad you're eating something," Clay stated, "but I am surprised to see you dressed for work. Taking a day off isn't a sign of weakness, you know."

"Says the man who opens the store no matter what," Emma added as she pulled a piece of crunchy cheese from the bowl with her fingers.

"I may not be the ideal example of it, but I do it for different reasons. You had a rough day today, Em. I'm sure Bernadette would understand."

"I have to go to work, Dad," Emma retorted. "I'll go stir-crazy if I just sit here and think about… it."

"You mean think about Noah," Clay corrected.

"No, not exactly," she said evasively, stirring her fork in the macaroni to swirl more cheese around.

"I'm not a doddering old fool, Emma," Clay said. "I saw the way you looked at each other and talked. I knew something was going on with you and Noah. That's why you wanted the whole day with him, alone."

Emma began to protest before her father shut her down.

"Hey, you don't have to deny it. You're a grown woman, Emma. You make your own decisions. I don't need or particularly want to know the details. It's okay for you to have feelings for him. You could do a lot worse than Noah Healy."

"I don't think it matters anyway, Dad," Emma said sadly as she finished her meal and rose from the table. She rinsed her bowl with hot water and turned back to face her father. "He's gone. He can't come back here any time soon, and who knows if I'll ever see him again."

"Don't give up hope just yet, Em," Clay said as he got up to grab the whistling tea kettle. "It's Christmas. Strange things can happen. It's magical."

"That sounded great when I was ten, Dad," Emma admitted. "I don't know about now."

Emma walked over and gave her father a kiss on the cheek.

"Thanks for trying, though."

Emma walked back into the dining room and saw her sister dive on top of whatever she was wrapping.

"Excuse me!" Hayley yelled. "This is a no entry without notification zone. Get out!"

"I'm going, I'm going," Emma replied, giving her mother a kiss on the cheek. "I'm leaving for work. See you in the morning."

"Be careful, honey," Alice requested.

Emma walked to the mudroom to grab her coat, boots, hat, and gloves before heading out into the night. The cold air had settled over the town once again, driving the temperature into the tens. Emma saw her breath hang in the air with each step taken. As she passed her father's shop and saw the sign noting just one shopping day left until Christmas, her heart was saddened. She put her head down and trudged on before bumping into someone just outside of the pub, sending her spinning to the sidewalk.

"Oh dear, I'm so sorry," an older voice said.

Emma looked up to see Mrs. Travers standing there with John, her caretaker.

"You okay, Emma?" John asked as he held out his hand to help Emma up.

"I'm fine," Emma replied, brushing off the snow from her pants and coat. "It was my fault. I wasn't looking up. I'm sorry, Mrs. Travers."

"Oh, there's nothing to be sorry about." Mrs. Travers smiled widely.

"She might be a little tipsy from her drinks," John whispered to Emma.

"I'm old, not deaf, John," Mrs. Travers scolded. "I may have had one too many sherries tonight, but who cares? It's the holidays, right, dear?"

"That's right." Emma smiled.

"Where's that handsome boyfriend of yours?" Mrs. Travers asked, looking around. "John, she is with such a lovely young man. He reminded me of my late husband in his younger days. So nice and friendly, and easy on the eyes too."

"Oh, he wasn't my boyfriend—not really," Emma said. "He's... he had to leave town."

"Right before Christmas? Oh, what a shame," Mrs. Travers added.

"Yes, yes, it is a shame."

"Come on, Mrs. Travers," John egged on, putting her arm through his. "Emma, you have a good night and a Merry Christmas."

"Thanks, John. You as well. And you too, Mrs. Travers," Emma said.

Mrs. Travers moved forward and gave Emma an embrace.

"You look like you could use a hug, dear," Mrs. Travers stated as she patted Emma's back.

"I could, thank you," Emma replied, feeling herself starting to cry.

"You know you are always my favorite person in this town," Mrs. Travers said quietly. "But don't tell anyone."

"I won't," Emma whispered back. She looked on as John led Mrs. Travers away to her car, getting her into the passenger seat so he could drive.

Emma paced the rest of the way to the hotel, standing outside the front door for a moment before building her resolve and entering.

Marianne stood behind the front desk and looked up as Emma moved closer to her.

"Emma! What are you doing here?"

"I'm coming to work like I always do," Emma said as she removed her knitted hat and gloves.

"I know. I just thought you weren't coming in after everything." Marianne made her way from around the front desk to stand next to Emma. "Emma," she said quickly and quietly, "you should probably go home. Bernadette and—"

Before Marianne could finish, Emma heard Bernadette's voice bellow from the back room.

"Marianne, is that Emma out there?" she yelled.

Marianne hesitated in answering.

"Yes, it's me," Emma spoke up.

"Emma, come to my office, please," Bernadette said stoically. "Marianne, can you get back to work?"

Emma stepped toward the back office, entering the room.

"Close the door," Bernadette ordered as she pointed to the seat in front of her desk. As Emma shut the door, it was then that she noticed Grace sitting in the office as well.

"What's up?" Emma asked.

"Seems like it's been a bit crazy here lately," Bernadette began.

"Bernadette, I didn't have anything to do with what went on upstairs," Emma started. "The fight was well underway before I got up there. Thankfully, I wasn't hurt at all."

"That you weren't the cause of all the damage isn't quite true, is it, Emma?" Bernadette asked.

"I don't know what you mean. The police report is pretty straightforward—"

"I'm not talking about all that," Bernadette said, shaking her head. "Grace told me you went up to Mr. Healy's room the other morning, and she didn't see you come back down."

"I went out the back door, and, not to be rude, Bernadette, but it's really none of your business or Grace's what I was doing. I was on my own time."

"That's fair," Bernadette agreed. "But what about this?"

Bernadette swung her computer screen around for Emma to look at. It was a security camera view from the office of Emma perched on the table, with Noah under her skirt.

Emma sat back in the chair, stunned.

"I'm not making excuses, Bernadette, but how is there a camera view to there? That camera is always pointed at the front desk."

"I guess I had repositioned it that morning—by mistake," Grace said.

"Do you have anything to say for yourself, Emma?" Bernadette said.

"All I can say is that I'm sorry. I should have used better judgment," Emma answered, not sure where things were going now.

"I'm shocked by all this, Emma," Bernadette added. "I had such high hopes for you with this company.

I'm going to have to ask you for your keys and your ID card and badge."

"You're firing me?"

"I don't really have a choice," Bernadette said, handing the keys directly over to Grace. "For now, Grace has agreed to take your shifts and will be interim night manager until I can get her into the corporate program. Don't worry. This video doesn't need to leave this room. I will be glad to provide you with a reference for a future job. Thank you for your service here."

Grace walked over and opened the office door, indicating it was time for Emma to go. Emma wanted to say something to Bernadette but held her tongue. Instead, she shot Grace a glare as she walked out of the office, and Grace closed the door behind her.

Emma went beyond the front desk and then turned toward the Christmas tree. She saw Marianne standing there, watching her. Marianne dashed over and gave Emma a hug.

"Emma, I'm so sorry. I had no idea they were doing this until they both came in a few minutes ago. I wanted to give you a heads-up, but—"

"It's not your fault, Marianne," Emma replied. "It was all mine. I have to own it."

"Except it's all on that bitch, Grace." Marianne snarled. "You know she moved that camera on purpose once she saw him with you."

"It doesn't matter," Emma resolved. "It's done, and I'm not sorry about it. I'll talk to you soon, Marianne. Have a good Christmas."

Emma strode across the lobby and went out the front door. She inhaled deeply several times to keep herself from choking up.

Emma began her walk back home, reaching the edge of the hotel and the alleyway that led up to the street. She saw Grace exit the side door and turn toward Emma.

"You should have known better," Grace shouted.

"Known better than what? To trust you? You're right about that," Emma answered. She had started to leave but then went back to confront Grace, moving down the alley and through the slush and ice.

"It had nothing to do with trust, Emma," Grace shot back.

"It's just funny that you repositioned that camera the same day you saw me walk in with Noah," Emma wondered aloud. "Oh, that's right. It was an accident."

"I'm not the one who let some guy go down on me while I was supposed to be working." Grace's eyes narrowed as she looked back at Emma.

"Think whatever you want, Grace," Emma dismissed. "I thought we were friends. I didn't realize you were just looking to step on me to move up the corporate ladder."

"Oh, please." Grace snarled. "You were always the golden child here who could do no wrong. Everyone just loves Emma. I worked twice as hard as you and never got any recognition. So yes, I saw an opportunity, and I took it. What I don't get is why someone like Noah Healy would choose you in the first place. You don't even know their music!"

"I'm sorry for you, Grace," Emma replied, turning to walk away. Emma heard a loud slam and turned after Grace had apparently kicked the door, slamming it with force. Emma looked back to see the avalanche of snow sliding off from the ledges above, dumping a healthy amount on top of Grace.

"Fuck!" Grace yelled out.

Snow had landed onto Grace's head and shoulders, enough that she had to shake it off like a dog coming in from the rain.

Emma kept moving forward, straining to suppress a laugh and a smile, as she worked her way back toward her house.

15

Noah spent most of the ride simply staring out the bus window, watching the world go by. When they had picked Ray up from the hospital, there was no conversation at all between the two of them. Noah took notice of the bruises on Ray's face and how gingerly he moved, and Ray barely glanced in Noah's direction when Jerry guided him onto the bus and to his bedroom in the back.

"Everyone all set?" Jerry said excitedly. "This is going to be great, guys!"

Jordan was the only one who seemed enthusiastic regarding the opportunity, while the others remained somewhat stone-faced.

"Geez, guys, it's not like we're going to a funeral here." Jerry pushed. "We're opening for the fucking Foo Fighters. They're Rock and Roll Hall of Famers. The place will be sold out and screaming."

"Yeah, for them, not us," Edgar said, twirling his drumsticks as he lay on his bunk. "No offense, Jerry. I love the opportunity to work at the same stage as them. But no one going to see them is going to care a bit that we're there."

"Well, it's your job to make them care," Jerry emphasized. "We get about an hour to bowl them over, so let's pick out our best cuts and play them."

"That pretty much eliminates anything we've done in the last six years," Pete added with a laugh.

"What are you talking about?" Jerry defended. "There were some good tracks on Diagnosis Slays.

"I think we have a different definition of what good is, Jerry," Edgar stated. "Right, Noah?"

All eyes turned to Noah, who sat still and looked out the window.

"Noah?" Edgar prodded.

Noah broke from his fog enough to reply.

"Eddie and Pete are right, Jerry," Noah said. "Everything after 2016 is shit. If we play any of that stuff, we'll just get booed off the stage. But hell, that might happen anyway."

"Nice to see you guys are so optimistic about this," Jerry answered, shaking his head. "Look, I've got to get back in my car. You guys have four or five hours together to work up a setlist before getting to the hotel. I told Foo Fighters' management we would have it to them by tonight. They just want to look it over and make sure—"

"Make sure it doesn't suck," Eddie interjected.

"Whatever." Jerry waved Eddie off. "Make sure you include Ray on the decisions."

A collective groan escaped the other bandmates' mouths.

"He's the one who has to sing them," Jerry noted.

Jerry departed the bus, allowing Noah to go back to staring out the window. Cecil guided the vehicle down Main Street, so they drove past the Birch residence once more. Noah looked over to see the bedroom light to Emma's room turned off. He wondered if she was home, how she felt, if Emma bothered to go to work, or if she cared he was leaving.

The long trek down the New York State Thruway provided little entertainment for Noah. However, he heard the occasional conversation among Jordan, Pete, and Eddie regarding the upcoming show. They even began to do a little acoustic jam of a few of their songs for early rehearsal, catching Noah's attention.

"What if we just do some covers and then a few of our songs sprinkled in?" Jordan asked.

"Because that's what Foo Fighters want ahead of them—some cover band they plucked out of a bar somewhere," Pete jibed. "We can't do that. So I say we play stuff off the first two albums only. We only have to do about forty minutes. Then, if we want, maybe we can do a cover song."

"The problem is going to be with Mr. Wonderful back there," Eddie said, lowering his voice. "You know how he gets. He will want to perform tracks off the last album like 'Do it Dirty' or 'Absolute Freak Show.' I hate those."

"Christmas," Noah shouted from the front of the bus.

"Oh, the zombie rises," Eddie replies. "What are you saying up there?"

Noah rose from his seat and turned toward the back of the bus where the three were sitting.

"We do some stuff off the first two albums that will take up most of the set. Then we sprinkle in a Christmas song at the end. It is a Christmas Day show, after all. I'm sure Foo Fighters are going to do at least one as well."

"That makes sense," Pete agreed. "Do you think we can convince Ray to do one? He's more of the Grinch type than Rudolph or Charlie Brown."

"If he doesn't sing one, I will," Noah asserted.

"Really?" Eddie answered.

"You can sing?" Jordan added.

He rubbed his temples, trying to control his temper.

"You know who wrote most of those songs on the first two albums?" Pete added, pointing at Noah.

"I know that, but... I don't know. I didn't know you sang lead," Jordan answered.

"I can," Noah said. "But we already have a lead singer. Ray and I may have our personal differences, but the truth is that he's a damn good singer. He took the lyrics and made them better. It's what he is best at. So I just stayed out of his way and let him do it. But, yes, Jordan, I can sing."

Noah took the lead in the conversation, helping to decide what five songs of theirs they would play that he knew Ray would agree to. They went back and forth on what Christmas song to include, talking about upbeat tunes like "Jingle Bell Rock" or "Here

Comes Santa Claus," before Noah made a suggestion.

"How about 'The Christmas Song'?"

"You mean the chestnuts roasting song?" Pete asked.

"Yeah. I like that one," Noah asked. "It's heavier on the piano, but I'm sure you guys can pick it up."

Noah reached over to the iPad sitting next to Jordan and went online to pull up the sheet music to show it to the rest of the band.

"I'm pretty sure I've never played it," Jordan said warily.

"Me neither," Eddie added.

"I have," Noah said confidently. "We can run through it and then do it at rehearsal to see how it sounds."

"See how what sounds?" Ray asked from the doorway of his room. Noah saw Ray stagger a bit as the bus rode before he reached one of the seats and sat down with the rest of the band.

"We're just talking about the setlist for the show," Eddie replied.

"Let me see it," Ray demanded.

Jordan passed the paper he had scrawled on to Ray. Ray flipped on the small overhead light over his seat so he could read it better. It also gave Noah a better look at the bruises and the mess he had made of Ray's face.

"How long of a set do we get to play?" Ray questioned.

"About forty minutes," Pete responded cautiously.

"I think we'll be short one song with this list," Ray said, passing the paper back to Jordan. "I like the choices, though. I think it will be good. I've never sung 'The Christmas Song.' I don't know if I could pull it off."

"I can do it," Noah said as he looked at Ray.

Ray nodded in agreement.

"Okay, you take it," Ray added. "We still need to come up with one more song."

Noah and the rest of the band sat stunned for a moment before snapping back to reality.

"Give me the night and let me see if I can come up with something," Noah answered.

"Something new?" Eddie said with shock.

"I have an idea. I just have to flesh it out some."

"Go do it," Ray said. Ray rose from his seat and went back to his bedroom, closing the accordion door behind him.

Noah looked at the remaining members of the band. No one seemed sure what to say or do.

"What the fuck was that?" Pete asked.

"Never mind what," Eddie said. "Who the fuck was that? Maybe you punched some sense into him, Noah. But, whatever it was, let's run with it before he hits his head and changes back."

Noah walked back toward the front of the bus and grabbed the empty passenger seat next to Cecil.

"Okay if I sit here for a bit?" Noah asked, pointing at the chair.

"Sure thing," Cecil answered. "I'm always up for company."

"No offense, Cecil, but I'm going to put my earbuds in to listen to music. I want to try to write something."

"No problem." Cecil smiled, returning to humming.

Noah slipped his earbuds in, putting Foo Fighters' *Skin and Bones* album on as he opened his journal. The first track, "Razor," kicked in, and Noah closed his eyes to listen. He was transported back to the fifteen-year-old when he first heard the CD and did his best to mimic the songs on his keyboard. Just hearing Dave Grohl's voice expertly move through the tune and the crowd's reaction along the way proved enough to drive Noah along when he was younger. Now, it might be just what he needed again.

Noah flipped the journal to the last page he wrote on that had "Emma" scrawled on the top. He put the nib of his pen on the first blank line and let it sit there for a moment, praying for inspiration. Then, as "Razor" transitioned from solo acoustic guitar to the whole band kicking in, raising the intensity and urgency of the song, including the background piano riff that stood out for Noah before hitting a frenetic crescendo to finish off the music, Noah flung his eyes open.

He placed his pen back on the top line and wrote the word "For" next to Emma and started to scribble down words like he hadn't in a long time.

By the time the bus had pulled up in front of the Plaza Hotel in Manhattan, Noah had written and rewritten several pages, with pages of lyrics crossed out and rearranged. He had placed some musical notes and ideas along the way to what he thought might sound best. He shut the journal as Cecil cut the engine for the bus and smiled.

"Man, you've been sitting there for hours scribbling," Cecil said in awe.

"I know," Noah acknowledged. "It felt great."

Noah stood up and stretched before exiting the bus, stepping out into the cold Manhattan night. The doorman at the hotel tipped his hat to Noah and pried the door open before he slipped inside to take in the luxurious atmosphere. The Plaza hosted legends—kings, presidents, dignitaries, the rich and famous—and here he was, among them, or at least their ghosts.

Naturally, the hotel was decked out in its holiday finery, with a beautiful Christmas tree as the centerpiece of the foyer. All Noah could think of was how impressed Emma would be with the look before him.

"Holy shit," Jordan said as he strode next to Noah. "This place is crazy."

"This is what big-time looks like, Junior," Eddie said as he walked up and put his arms around Noah and Jordan.

"Remember the days of swanky hotels, Noah?" Eddie smiled.

"It seems like forever ago, but yeah, I do," Noah answered.

"Savor it while you can, Jordan," Noah advised. "You don't know how long it's going to last."

Noah saw Jerry approaching them as they stood in the foyer.

"You guys made it!" Jerry said with excitement. "I've got us all checked in. You guys," he said, pointing to Pete, Eddie, and Noah, "have the Tower Suite. Jordan, sorry, but you just get a junior suite."

"Seems fitting for Junior," Pete joked.

"I don't care," Jordan stated. "Just getting to say I stayed here will blow my family away. But, speaking of family, Jerry... is there any way to score some tickets to the show? I've got a ton of people who will come."

"We each get six comp tickets," Jerry told him. "No more than that, and even those were tough to get. I'll get them to you tomorrow."

"Six?" Jordan bemoaned. "Man, I have like twelve people who want to come!"

"Don't worry, Junior," Pete comforted Jordan. 'You can have some of mine—for a price, of course."

Ray walked up, and Jerry ran to greet him as Noah and the others looked on.

"Ray, how are you feeling? Everything good? Do you need something?" Jerry fawned over Ray.

"What room am I in?" Ray asked bluntly, wearing sunglasses to hide his black eyes.

"I was able to get you the Fitzgerald King Suite," Jerry beamed. "It's luxury to the max."

"What room do you have?" Ray asked Jordan.

"I've got one of the junior suites," Jordan answered.

"I'll take Junior's room," Ray said. "He can have the King Suite."

"What?" Jerry said, dumbfounded. "You know how much that room costs a night? It's super plush, Ray. Right up your alley."

"Been there, done that," Ray said. "Let the kid have it. Where are you at?" he said, turning to Noah.

"The Tower Suite with Pete and Eddie," Noah replied.

"You get anything?" Ray said, pointing to Noah's journal.

"I did, I think," Noah told him, tapping the journal.

"Mind if I come up and take a look at it when you're settled?"

"Sure." Noah nodded.

Ray walked off toward the elevators, getting a few yards away before he turned back.

"Jerry, you coming so I can get into my room?"

"Yeah, sure, Ray," Jerry said as he scrambled away from the group.

"Does Ray have an unknown twin that they could have switched him with at the hospital?" Eddie asked. "You know, like the nice one instead of the evil one?"

"I don't care what happened." Jordan smiled. "All I know is I'm staying in a King Suite!"

Noah and the others went to their suite, each selecting one of the luxury bedrooms available. The rooms were immense, with views of Fifth Avenue and all the holiday glitter below the city. Noah glanced at his watch and saw it was nearly two in the morning. He imagined Emma sitting behind the front desk working right now at the Emerald Lake Hotel. His desire to contact her rose, but he held off calling the hotel or texting her, unsure of what the outcome might be if he did.

A knock on the suite door had Pete dashing over to get it.

"I hope that's the food I ordered. I'm starving after living off diner food for days."

Pete opened the door and saw Ray standing there. Noah walked out of his bedroom to see what was going on.

"Just Ray," Pete said with disappointment.

Noah and Ray met in the living room area, sitting down on the plush chairs in the room.

"Pete," Eddie said, "come with me to my room. I want to show you the view I have there from my balcony. You can see all up down Fifth."

"Big deal," Pete said. "I want my food."

"Get over here. The food will be here soon enough," Eddie said, gritting his teeth and waving Pete over until he understood what he was getting at.

"Yeah, sure," Pete said begrudgingly as he walked to Eddie's room and closed the door behind him.

"How's your room?" Noah asked Ray, trying to break the ice.

"It's fine." Ray nodded, fiddling with his sunglasses. "A lot better than some of the real shitholes we have stayed in over the years."

"It was nice of you to give your suite to Jordan," Noah indicated.

"Well, Junior hasn't had the chance to experience what it was like when we were on top, you know? So he might as well get a taste of it while we have the chance, right?"

"It was still a good thing to do. Although I have to admit, it surprised the hell out of all of us."

Ray reached up and removed his sunglasses, showing the dark purple and blue that covered both eyes and his nose.

"Yeah, I've had a lot of things surprise me over the last day or so," Ray told Noah. "Like how good of a fighter you are when you get worked up."

"Look, Ray," Noah started before Ray held up his hand.

"Don't even go there, Noah," Ray interrupted. "I know it was all on me. I think I just needed the ass-kicking to bring it out. You guys should have done that a long time ago."

"I'm pretty sure at least one of us has wanted to at any given time for the last few years."

"All I can say is"—Ray took a deep breath—"I'm sorry. I know I'm an asshole sometimes—probably most of the time. You guys let me get away with a lot of shit you shouldn't have, and I know you did it for the group. I'm sorry if I fucked things up with that girl. That wasn't cool what I said or did. You should have kicked me around some more."

"I would have if the cop didn't Taser me." Noah laughed.

"Good, good," Ray said, nodding more. "I'm gonna try to be better, Noah. I know I've got a lot of work to do and stuff to make up for. All I can tell you is that I'll work at it. I know this is your band at heart."

"Fair enough," Noah answered. "But it's not just my band. It's all of us. It was never supposed to be about one person."

Silence hung in the air for a moment before Ray pointed to the worn journal sitting on Noah's lap.

"Can I take a look at your song?"

"Yeah, sure," Noah said, handing over the journal. "I think it might be kind of rough still."

Ray read it over, mouthing some of the words as he went, trying to catch the melody that Noah went for.

"It's good." Ray smiled. "I would change the refrain a bit. Make this word 'overdue,' and it flows better."

"Yeah, yeah, I like that," Noah said as he scribbled out the change in his journal.

"One other thing about it," Ray indicated. "I think you should sing it at the show."

"Nah, you're the singer, Ray," Noah said as he shut the journal. "I gave up the lead when we knew how good you were. Backup works just fine for me."

"Not for this one, it doesn't," Ray told him. "It's got to come from you, Noah. You need to own this one. It's pretty fucking good."

"Okay," Noah agreed. "Thanks, Ray."

"No problem. Now go get some sleep. It's going to be a long day tomorrow."

Another knock resounded loudly on the door to the suite. Pete came dashing out of Eddie's room to answer the door.

"Sorry to break up the lovefest out here," Pete said as he ran by. "I'm too fucking hungry to wait anymore."

Pete opened the door to let the butler in with the food he ordered, and Ray plucked a pile of grapes off the tray as he walked out of the room.

16

Christmas Eve morning tolled in with Emma tucked away in her bed. Incessant knocking on her bedroom door finally caused her to peek her head out from underneath her blanket.

"What?" she yelled.

Hayley walked in smiling, holding a mug of coffee.

"Merry Christmas Eve, sunshine," she said to her sister.

"Ugh. What's so merry about it?"

Emma pulled the blanket back over her head while Hayley walked over and opened the curtains and window shade to Emma's window.

"It's a beautiful day out, Emma," Hayley began as she placed the mug down on Emma's nightstand. Then she peeled back the blanket, leaving Emma scrambling on the bed, looking for something to cover up with.

"No, sunlight bad. Darkness good," Emma grunted as she placed a pillow over her head.

"Will you stop it," Hayley said, tugging on the pillow. "What are you just going to wallow around for the entire holiday?"

"I'm allowed to wallow," Emma said as she sat up. "I lost my job, Noah left, and I'll probably never see him again. So there's nothing to look forward to right now."

"We're supposed to make Christmas cookies today," Hayley reminded her. "It's tradition. Mom is already all pumped about it. She made me go out and get extra ingredients. Besides, Dad was looking for you too."

"What does he want?"

"He wanted to know if you could come down to the store and help him out. He said he's swamped. He also said not to put up with pouting and the 'poor Emma' routine."

"You have got to be kidding me," Emma gruffed as she got out of bed.

"It's not like you have anything better to do today anyway, right?" Hayley grinned slyly.

"Get out!" Emma shouted, tossing a pillow at her sister as Hayley scooted out the door.

Emma sat on the edge of her bed before getting up and looking at herself in the mirror. She had returned home last night, explained getting fired to her parents, and hid in the darkness of her room for hours, moving between anger and sorrow. Now, with her hair disheveled and feeling glum, the last thing she wanted to do was get ready to go and work with the public, where she would have to put on a happy holiday face and smile all day.

The ring of her phone made her jump, and she excitedly moved to her nightstand, hoping it might be Noah reaching out to her even though he wasn't supposed to do so. However, disappointment overcame her when she saw it was her father.

"Hi, Dad," she answered.

"Hey, honey," Clay told her. "Try not to sound so excited that it's me."

"I'm sorry, it's not you. It's just—"

"I know, I know," Clay said. "Anyway, did Hayley give you my message? I could sure use your help down here. People are cleaning me out for last-minute gifts."

"Yeah, just let me get dressed, and I'll be down in a few minutes," she said gloomily.

"That's the Christmas spirit. I think," Clay answered. "See you in a bit."

Emma dressed quickly, putting on jeans and a cheery red sweatshirt, tied her hair in a ponytail, and headed downstairs. She walked through the kitchen, spotting Hayley and her mother hard at work at cookie making. The smell of baking ginger wafted through, catching Emma's attention.

"Smells great, Mom," Emma said as she sat and put her boots on.

"Grandma's recipe for ginger snaps is always the best one." Alice smiled. "Where are you off to?"

"Dad needs help at the store," Emma moaned.

Oh, well, at least it will help take your mind off... things," Alice said, returning to placing gobs of dough down and then pressing out sugar cookies.

"It's hard to keep my mind off those things if everyone keeps mentioning him—I mean, them!" Emma said as she struggled with the zipper on her coat. "Now this goddamn zipper is stuck!"

"Emma Louise Birch, language please!" her mother scolded.

Hayley walked over to assist Emma, working on the jammed zipper to pull the fabric out.

"Trust me, you're better off going to work with Dad today," Hayley whispered. "I've been shopping and making cookies since seven this morning."

"Hayley, get the ginger snaps out before they burn!" Alice shouted.

"Aye, aye, Captain," Hayley said as she unjammed Emma's jacket. "Have fun," she said, kissing Emma's cheek.

Emma walked out the back door and was enveloped in the sunshine. Trees were shedding their icicles and weighted piles of snow so the constant dripping could be heard as she moved along toward the Birch Tree. She expected to see a crowd of people coming to and going from the shop when she got to the front door, but when she pulled the door open, one lone customer was looking through a rack of jackets that hung near the front and were on sale.

Emma moved over to the front counter, where her father was positioned by the register.

"Oh good, you made it here," Clay said.

"Dad, you told me you were swamped down here," Emma said, looking around the store. "Where are the customers?"

"Oh, you just missed the last wave," Clay replied. "It was crazy in here, though, wasn't it, Mrs. Winston?" Clay shouted to the woman looking at the jackets.

"Oh yes," she said without missing a beat. "Wall to wall people. That's why I waited so long to start looking."

"Thanks for rushing down, honey," Clay said, hugging Emma's shoulders from behind.

"No problem." Emma sighed as her father went to the office.

Mrs. Winston approached, holding a forest green jacket, and placed it on the counter.

"Do you think Ronnie will like this?" Mrs. Winston said, referring to her son in college.

Emma held up the jacket, noticing that it was a 3XL.

"It seems a little big for Ronnie," Emma noted, remembering what he looked like when she saw him in the summer.

"Oh, well, he's put on a little at school," Mrs. Winston said. "You know how boys can be. By the way, Emma, Ronnie isn't seeing anyone right now. I mean, if you're looking for someone to hang out with at the pub or go to a movie with."

Emma cringed inside, feeling like her entire personal life was now on display for the town of Emerald Lake.

"Oh, thanks, Mrs. Winston," Emma said, stuffing the jacket inside a gift box. "I think I'm pretty busy right now. But give Ronnie my best."

"Oh, okay," Mrs. Winston answered, taking her package. "It's just that I heard you lost your job at the hotel and might want some company."

Emma maintained her composure and smiled.

"I'm okay, thank you," Emma said. "You have a Merry Christmas."

Mrs. Winston left the store as Clay walked out from the back.

"Dad, I can't do this all day," Emma complained. "Everyone in town knows my business right now and is sure to mention. Mrs. Winston wants to set me up with Ronnie and knows I lost my job."

"You know how things are here, Em," Clay answered. "Small-town gossip. People latch onto anything they can to pass the time. Ronnie's a nice guy."

"You're missing the point, Dad," Emma said, frustrated. Finally, she took notice of her father zipping on his coat. "What are you doing?"

"What do you mean?"

"Why are you putting your coat on?" Emma questioned.

"Oh, I have some errands to run," Clay said. "Mrs. Travers needs me to deliver some packages out to her, and then I have some inventory to check out. I also have some shopping of my own to do."

"You had me come down here because you were busy, and now you're leaving me alone in the store?"

"Look around, Emma," Clay said, waving his hands. "The place is dead. Nick promised to drop off some lunch for you at noon, and you can close up at four if I'm not back by then. Thanks for helping out."

Clay planted a kiss on Emma's cheek and rushed out the door, leaving Emma standing and wondering what had happened.

"Merry Christmas to me," she grumbled as she pulled on the Santa hat left on the counter.

****

Noah and the rest of the band took a limo over to Madison Square Garden to check out the space for the concert and do a run-through of their songs before they would do a full rehearsal the morning of the show. The band was let in through security and came up backstage before walking out and see how the arena was configured.

"Oh, man," Jordan said in awe. "This is amazing. Have you guys ever played here before?"

Noah soaked in the atmosphere, looking for a hint of familiarity.

"Back in 2011, we opened for Florence + the Machine," Noah recalled. "Then, in 2013, we headlined two shows here. Remember that, Eddie?"

"Boy do I," Eddie answered. "It was nuts. The place was rocking. You could hardly hear yourself think."

Eddie looked back as the roadies unloaded the new pieces of his drum kit to replace what was damaged in the truck accident while Pete and Jordan moved to check out the setups for their guitars. Noah moved toward the edge of the stage and looked out at all the empty seats.

"Pretty amazing to be back here," Ray said as he slapped Noah's back.

"I gotta be honest," Noah said as he turned around. "I never thought it would happen again."

"Everything happens for a reason," Ray said, taking off his sunglasses.

"That's what they tell me," Noah said quietly, recalling the words Emma had spoken to him.

Noah stepped over to his piano, running his hand over the wood and feeling the familiarity of it before gliding to the keys. He ran scales to make sure it was in tune and undamaged from the accident, and it sounded as perfect as ever. Calm settled over Noah in a way it hadn't for a while as he sat down on the wooden bench before the piano as he began to play, driving into one of his songs with a thunder. He lifted his hands from the keys and smiled, looking back at his bandmates.

"I'm ready," Noah stated.

Noah looked on as Eddie climbed behind his drum kit and Pete and Jordan took up their positions on the stage. Ray sat down on a stool, creating an informal circle among the band as they began to rehearse, playing four or five songs as they wrangled over what the best approach would be to each one, where it should come in the set, and if they should try something different. Noah filled with excitement as he knew they had become more like a band than they had been for several years.

"I think we should switch out 'Dead Locked' and sing 'Coming Home' instead," Ray added.

"You always hated that song," Pete replied with surprise. "I don't think we've played that one live since we released the album."

"Then it's time to bring it out," Ray added. "It just seems to fit right now."

"I don't think I've ever played that one," Jordan added as the junior member of the band.

"Follow me, Jordan," Noah indicated.

Noah nodded and began the intro to the song, a soft piano melody that he closed his eyes for. Jordan picked up his acoustic guitar and strummed along before picking up where Noah was going. Ray sang expertly like he had sung it a hundred times over.

When they had finished playing, Noah grinned over at Ray.

"We should open with that," Noah said, with the rest of the band agreeing.

"Only if we close with your new song," Ray emphasized.

"I don't know," Noah replied warily.

"Wait, there's a new song?" Eddie asked.

"Noah wrote it last night. It's perfect, and I think he needs to sing it."

"Can we hear it?" Pete and Jordan asked in unison before staring at each other and laughing.

"Come on, man, play it," Ray egged on.

Noah shook his head and sighed before agreeing. He did the piano player cliché of cracking his knuckles to get a laugh from the band before he started playing. Those first few notes were filled with nerves, just as if Noah were that ten-year-old playing his first recital. The music filled him in a way songs usually didn't, and he surprised even himself when he didn't have to look at the words or the sheet music, and the song just came naturally. With his eyes closed, he envisioned singing the song to Emma.

Noah opened his eyes as he completed playing and saw the rest of the band staring at him.

"Okay, let me have it," Noah said, preparing for the criticism from his friends.

"I guess I'll start," Eddie said, stepping forward. He stared at Noah with a stern look.

"Nah, I can't do it, man," Eddie burst out laughing. "It was great. I think I can add some soft drums to it, maybe with the brushes."

"I've definitely got some bass ideas we can play with," Pete said, "but I freakin' loved it, man. Nice work."

The band worked and reworked the song, kicking ideas back and forth until they had something everybody agreed was ideal. Noah even found Ray joining in with light tambourine play as the song went along.

It wasn't until a couple of the road crew stepped out on stage to let them know their time ended that the band stopped playing. Noah closed the piano and sat back, sipping the bottle of water he had on stage with him.

"Great work today," Ray complimented Noah. "We're gonna surprise the hell out of them tomorrow."

"I think so too," Noah said. Excitement coursed through him, and he rose from the piano, turning to walk offstage.

Noah stepped down off the side of the stage and heard his name get called out. He spun around and saw Clay Birch standing there.

Noah walked swiftly over to Clay to greet him.

"Clay, what the hell are you doing here?" Noah asked.

"I haven't been into the city for a long time, so I thought I would check things out and see what it was like. You know, sightseeing, shopping, maybe taking in a show. What do you think?"

"I think you're nuts," is what Noah replied. "We can both get in trouble for you being here."

"No, we can't. I don't work for the hotel, and I'm not Emma. We're fine. Besides, I don't see any Emerald Lake cops around here."

"So what are you really doing here then, Clay?"

"Do you really need me to explain all that to you?" Clay questioned.

Clay placed his hand on Noah's shoulder.

"You'll find out someday when you're a parent, Noah, that your kids are the most essential thing in the world to you. Then you'll do whatever you have to so that they are happy with life. Right now, Emma is far from that. She feels pretty distraught over everything that has happened. I hate to see one of my girls like that, whatever the reason. But it's my job as the father to try to fix it. That's why I'm here."

"How did you even find me or get in here in the first place?"

Clay chuckled at the question.

"What, do you think because I live in Nowhere, New York, I don't know people? I've been around a long time, Noah. So I took that business card your friend Mr. Martin left with Emma and called his office. I sweet-talked the gal who answered, and she let me know where you were. After that, well, Nick Klaus knows one of the higher-ups here at the Garden, so he got me a way in with the security guards as long as I didn't wander around too much. That was a beautiful song you played at the end there."

"You… you heard that, huh?" Noah asked, shuffling his feet.

"I did, but I don't think I'm the one you should care about hearing it."

"I don't know what to do about any of it, Clay. I hate that I had to leave, especially like I did. It's tearing me up," Noah lamented.

"Well, let's see what we can do about all of that," Clay offered. "I have a few ideas that might get you pointed in the right direction. The only problem is that we need to work quickly. The Christmas magic runs out pretty soon."

"What?" Noah said, confused by the statement.

"Geez, Noah, didn't you watch any of those cartoons when you were growing up? You've got a lot of catching up to do about a lot of things."

****

Emma closed up the shop without much fanfare, getting a few sales spread throughout the day, but mostly just getting people coming in to say hello or find out if the gossip they heard about her was true. She mostly tried to evade the questions, acknowledging that she was gone from the hotel without getting into any of the gory details.

Once she got home, Emma heard waves of Christmas music and singing. Her senses were bombarded with the smell of warm cookies in the air, and no sooner had she entered the house when her sister had Emma's coat off and an apron on her, so she got swept up in a frenzy as well. The baking efforts proved to be just the tonic Emma needed, letting her put aside the troubles she had faced over the last twenty-four hours and become rekindled by the magic of Christmas.

Dinner time rolled around and, still, with no signs of Clay anywhere, Emma became concerned with her father's whereabouts. The traditional Birch Christmas Eve meal of pastrami sandwiches and French fries, unusual by some family standards, was all but finished with preparation and the table set. Emma glanced out the front window once more and saw no truck in the driveway.

"Where do you think he is?" she asked with worry.

"I'm sure he's fine," Alice reassured her as she brought out the mustard and homemade pickles to the dining room table.

"Aren't you worried even a little bit, Mom?" Emma said as she spun around. "He hasn't answered his cell phone or returned texts or anything."

"Emma, you are worrying over nothing," Alice said, moving her wheelchair over to the living room. "You know your father. He probably got caught up in helping Paul Gibson cut down his Christmas tree on the farm and drag it into the house. Once he does that, you know they'll be sitting around drinking coffee or going to the diner for time with the guys. He could be doing a thousand other things. It's just him. I stopped worrying about it a long time ago."

"He probably started yapping with his cronies at the pub and completely forgot the time," Hayley added as she entered the dining room with the platter of hot pastrami. "Emma, can you grab your rye bread from the kitchen?"

Emma nodded, only partly paying attention, as she continued to be concerned about her father. Emma picked up the loaves of homemade rye bread, the bread just slightly warm from recent baking, as she placed them on the wooden cutting board and grabbed a bread slicing knife. Hayley followed her into the kitchen to pull the French fries from the oven.

"Mom's being kind of casual about Dad being so late," Emma noted.

"I think you're worrying too much," Hayley commented as she closed the oven door with her hip.

"Why are you both being so cavalier about it?" Emma said, raising her voice. "It's Christmas Eve, and he's been gone all day. What if he got in an accident? With the roads outside of town, his truck could have slipped off the road and into a ditch somewhere that no one would find for a week."

"Nice image to have on Christmas, Em," Hayley said.

"But it's true," she insisted, carrying the bread into the dining room.

"What's true?" Alice asked.

"Oh, Emma has read one too many horror novels and is overdramatizing," Hayley dismissed. "Dad will walk through that door any second once the smell of pastrami reaches the front porch."

At that moment, a thud was heard on the front porch before the door swung open. Clay brushed off his jacket and walked to the dining room, taking the coat off and placing it on the back of his chair at the head of the table. He reached for two slices of bread and the plate of pastrami as the three women stared at him.

"Okay, that was creepy," Emma said.

"What?" Clay asked as he fed a piece of pastrami into his mouth.

"Nothing, just an Emma freak-out," Hayley said as she munched on a pickle. "Good pickles, Em."

"Where have you been all day?" Emma asked her father as everyone began passing plates of food.

"I told you, I was running errands and doing stuff today. So that's why I needed you at the store," Clay answered. "Thank you for doing that, by the way. How was it?"

"Dead most of the day, which is what I was beginning to think about you. I tried calling you and texting you a bunch of times, and you never answered."

"I'm sorry about that, Em," Clay said sincerely. "I kept leaving my phone in the truck going in and out. You know Paul Gibson and that dang tree every year. He waits until the last minute and can't drag it in by himself. Laura made coffee after that, and I just lost track of time."

"I told you," Alice said, looking at Emma as she munched her sandwich.

"Fine, but you could have called," Emma spoke, finally accepting the answer.

The family started eating, enjoying the meal, and laughing as Frank Sinatra crooned in the background. The fun broke up when Clay's cell phone went off. He reached into his pocket and pulled the phone out, answering it immediately.

"Sure, that one he answers right away," Emma said with a frown.

The family began to clear the table as Clay stepped away to take his call, bringing dishes to the kitchen and putting things away before Clay came in.

"That was Mrs. Travers," Clay announced. "I need to take a ride to her house. I guess John forgot a couple of things for Christmas that she needs from the store."

"I can go with you," Emma offered as she placed dishes in the dishwasher.

"No, no, it's fine," Clay said. "I'll just be a few minutes, honest. You guys stay here where it's warm. Maybe you can make me some of your famous brownies, so they're nice and warm when I get back, with some hot cocoa?"

"Really, Dad?" Emma answered. "We just made about five hundred cookies all day today, and you want brownies?"

"You know your mother ends up giving away most of the cookies to the neighbors," Clay told her. "And I do love brownies. So consider it your Christmas present to me."

"I thought working at the store all day today was going to be your Christmas present."

"No, I'll pay you for that," Clay answered. "It was an honest day of work. This is special."

"Fine," Emma huffed. "But you better be back here by the time they get out of the oven."

"I promise," Clay said, crossing his heart. Clay walked over and gave Alice a kiss before getting ready to go. "I'll be back quickly, I swear. Maybe you guys can bring the presents out before I get back and put them under the tree."

"Geez, Dad, anything else you want us to do today?" Hayley complained. "Sweep the floor, do the dishes, make me brownies, get the presents. We're just like Cinderellas."

"Yes, you are," Clay said, hugging Hayley and Emma at the same time. "My princesses. All three of you," he added, smiling at Alice.

"Aww, that's sweet." Alice beamed. She reached into the side pocket of her wheelchair and grabbed her cell phone to snap a quick picture of Clay with his girls, Clay smiling widely while the girls grimaced.

Emma set to work mixing up the brownies, adding a generous portion of Cara Sel caramel to them before settling them into the oven to bake. She pulled out the container of homemade hot cocoa mix she put together, along with the marshmallows she created to look like snowmen and had stored earlier, placing them on a large platter with Santa Claus mugs.

True to his word this time, Clay came into the house as Emma pulled the brownies from the oven about forty minutes later. She placed the hot pan of brownies on a separate tray before getting the hot milk for the cocoa.

"Oh, I can smell them already," Clay said, clapping his hands.

"Everything okay with Mrs. Travers? "Emma asked as she took some whipped cream out of the fridge.

"Hmm? Oh, yeah, no problems at all," Clay said as he was caught attempting to pry the hot corner piece of a brownie right from the tray.

"Give me two seconds, and I'll cut them, Dad," Emma scolded.

"It's more fun this way," he added as he placed a piece of the warm, fudgy cake into his mouth, steam coming out as he did.

Clay helped Emma carry the treats into the living room, where Hayley had just finished arranging the presents just like Alice wanted them, so the tree looked its best. Next, Clay dimmed the lights around the house, so the glow came primarily from the Christmas tree and the fireplace as everyone sat down.

Emma cut and served out brownies before pouring hot cocoa for everyone, with each choosing their own toppings. Emma laughed loudly as Clay heaped whipped cream onto his brownie to the point where it covered his nose each time he took a bite.

"I don't care. It's delicious, Em." Clay smiled.

Emma glanced at the clock on the mantle, noticing it was approaching midnight.

"One more tradition before midnight," Clay said. Emma saw him reach to the side of his recliner and pull the Bible out of the pouch. He flipped to the familiar passage in the Book of Luke that the family read each Christmas Eve, passing the book around so each of them could read a line aloud relating to the birth of Jesus. When Emma completed the final lines and handed the Bible to her father, he closed the book and smiled.

Emma then walked over to the Christmas tree, plucked one of the candy canes off, and moved to the fireplace where the stockings hung. Next, she walked to the handmade stockings her mother had made when each of them was born and stopped at the one on the end that had Paul's name on it. She placed the single candy cane inside, hooking it on the top.

"Merry Christmas, big brother," she whispered.

17

All Emma could think to herself when she heard the knocks on her door on Christmas morning was that she needed to get back to work so that Hayley would stop interrupting her sleep. Emma peered one eye out at her alarm clock and saw it was barely seven in the morning.

"Hayley, you're not six anymore. We don't have to get up this early on Christmas," she yelled.

Hayley popped the door open, her hair everywhere, and her eyes barely open herself.

"It wasn't me who did it," Hayley groaned as she plopped down on the bed next to Emma. "It was Dad." Hayley curled up under the blanket next to her sister as the two of them lay there. The two rested softly together before Clay knocked on the door.

"Come on, you two, it's Christmas morning!" Clay chirped. The echoes of Christmas music rang through the house.

"Dad, it's too early," Emma moaned.

"What she said," Hayley agreed, putting the pillow over her head.

"You two used to dash into our bedroom before the sun came up on Christmas morning, begging to open presents."

"We didn't realize how wonderful sleep was at the time," Emma answered.

"Your mom is waiting downstairs," Clay told his daughters. "You know how she loves Christmas mornings."

"Really, Dad? Playing the guilt card? That's pretty low," Emma said as she sat up.

Emma got out of bed, her feet hitting the cold wood floor before she put on her slippers and got into her gray robe that hung on the back of her bedroom door. She realized the last time she had put the robe on was when Noah was with her and saddened before turning back toward her bed, where Hayley still lay under the blankets.

"Let's go, Hayley," Emma said, shoving her sister's feet.

"Just go and open my presents and tell me what I got later," Hayley said, her voice muffled under the pillow."

"If I'm up, you're up," she said, pulling the blanket down.

"Fine, but I better find a lump of coal in your stocking, Dad, for making us do this!" Hayley shouted as she got out of bed.

Emma and her sister made their way down the stairs to the living room. When they arrived, Alice snapped two quick pictures of the girls standing there.

"Mom!" Hayley yelled, covering her face.

"Oh, you two look so cute." Alice laughed.

"That better not end up on Facebook," Hayley warned.

"Merry Christmas, Mom," Emma said as she walked over and gave her mother a hug and a kiss. "Is there—"

"Yes, your father made coffee already." Alice nodded.

"Thank God," Emma grumbled as she staggered toward the kitchen to get a mug. When she returned, having taken a sip to revive her senses, she saw her father sitting in his recliner while Hayley sat on the couch. Emma curled up next to

Hayley, pulling one of the throw blankets down onto her lap.

"Hayley, you need to dole out the presents," Clay stated.

"Come on, Dad," Hayley whined. "I do it every year."

"Tradition says the youngest in the family does it," Clay said authoritatively.

"So I'll be doing this forever?" she questioned.

"At least until we have some grandkids," Alice said with a smile.

"Don't look at me," Emma said when all eyes turned to her as she went to sip her coffee. "I don't even have any prospects."

"Don't say that," Alice added. "You never know if Noah—"

"Mom, please," Emma interrupted. "I don't want to think about it today."

Hayley went about passing out gifts until each person had their small pile.

"Okay, Alice, you start," Clay said, pointing to his wife.

"So not only do I have to pass out all the gifts forever, but I always have to wait until last to open mine too! Boy, I love family traditions," Hayley complained.

Everyone opened their gifts in turn, with wrapping paper covering the floor. Emma received a couple of the cookbooks she had hoped for, along with a necklace from Hayley that had a heart on it engraved "Sisters 4 Eva."

Clay sat back in his recliner when all the presents were opened, drinking his coffee and rocking gently. Emma and Hayley looked at each other and then looked at their father, waiting to mouth the words he always said.

"Well, all that running around, and it's over that fast," Clay said as his daughters mimicked him and laughed.

"Oh, wait," Clay interrupted, standing up. "It's not quite over yet." He walked over to Hayley and Emma and handed them each an envelope. "One last gift."

Both girls looked questioningly at the plain white envelopes. Hayley tore hers open first and looked inside.

"No freakin' way!" she squealed.

"Hayley Marie!" Alice exclaimed.

"I didn't swear, Mom," Hayley noted. "Is this real?"

Emma opened her envelope to see what was inside. In it was a ticket to a concert and it said Foo Fighters on it.

"Who are they?" Emma asked.

"Oh my God, Emma, you are not coming," Hayley said with an eye roll. "They've been around for twenty-five years. They are one of the best rock bands of all time. I've always wanted to see them."

"Yes, Emma is going with us," Clay said as he held up a third ticket.

"You're going too?" Hayley said in disbelief.

"Who do you think is driving you two there?"

"I assumed we would take the bus or the train," Hayley said.

"What about Mom?" Emma asked. "We can't just leave her here on Christmas."

"It's okay, honey," Alice assured her. "Your father has already arranged everything. Marianne, Gary, and the kids are coming over to keep me company for a bit, and then Nick and Eileen will be here for dinner. So I will be fine."

"I thought it would be a nice way to spend the day with my girls," Clay said. We'll go see the Rockefeller Center tree, walk around the city, grab some dinner and then go to the show."

"When are we leaving?" Hayley said excitedly.

"As soon as you two who didn't want to get up can get yourselves ready to leave." Clay laughed.

"Emma, get your butt in gear," Hayley ordered. "I want to get going."

Hayley dashed over to her father and gave him a big hug before racing up the stairs. Emma walked over and hugged her father.

"Thanks, Dad. It's really sweet of you, even if I have no idea who they are."

"We've got hours in the car to get down there," Clay said. "I'm sure Hayley will make sure you know their music by the time we get there, so we don't embarrass her."

Emma rushed through dressing, putting on some jeans and a long-sleeved T-shirt before putting her hair in a ponytail.

"Emma, come on!" Hayley yelled impatiently from the bottom of the stairs.

"I'm going as fast as I can," Emma said as she plodded down the steps.

"Every extra minute you take is one less we get to spend in the city," Hayley answered, handing Emma her coat.

The girls climbed into Clay's truck, with Hayley sliding into the smaller back seat while Emma sat up in front. Hayley insisted on streaming all Foo Fighters music for the trip. She spent the first several hours on the road singing every song loudly and giving Emma and her father background information about the band. It wasn't until they had hit the Harriman area on the Thruway that Hayley fell asleep, and Emma took the opportunity to turn the music down.

"You're going to be able to sit through a whole concert of hard rock music, Dad?" Emma questioned.

"I'll be fine." Clay smiled, holding up earplugs that he often used when cutting trees down. He passed an extra pair to Emma. "You might want them. Our seats are close to the stage."

"Why are you doing this?" Emma asked as she looked out the window. She saw four or five emerald green motorcycles roar past the truck and down the highway.

"Because I wanted to do something with you two," Clay told her. "You girls are getting older. Hayley will be off to college next year, and you... who knows what great things you will be off doing by then. This might be one of the few times we have left to take a trip like this."

"I don't think I'm going anywhere anytime soon," Emma said as she leaned her head against the window.

"You don't know that, Em," Clay replied. "A lot can happen in a short period. Look at what happened just a few days ago. Noah got stuck here and all of a sudden—"

"Please, Dad," Emma answered. "I don't want to talk about Noah."

"Okay, but my point is, things can spin around at any moment. You could be anywhere, and something turns your life around. Did I ever tell you how your mother and I got together?"

"Plenty of times," Emma said. "You met in high school."

"Yes, we met in high school, but we didn't date in high school," Clay explained. "Back then, your mom was working for the Perry Company as an admin assistant while I worked with my father at the store. It was around Christmas time, and Perry was holding their Christmas party at the Monteverde, that Italian restaurant that used to be in town. It was the swankiest place in the area. She complained about it, saying she didn't want to go alone to another holiday party and asked me if I wanted to go with her. Of course, I said yes. We went and danced and had a good time. When I drove her home afterward, she leaned over and gave me a kiss good night. We were hooked after that."

"So Mom asked you out first?" Emma said with surprise.

"Technically, yes," Clay agreed.

"And she kissed you first?"

"I suppose you could say that."

"Way to go, Mom." Emma giggled.

"The point of the story is that your life can change in an instant like that," Clay spoke up. "You don't know who or what is going to come along that can be the reason things go your way. Fate can be funny that way."

Yeah, fate is funny, Emma thought, considering what brought her and Noah together in the first place.

About five hours after the trip had begun, Clay pulled into a parking garage in Manhattan. The girls excitedly climbed out and walked into the daylight of the city, taking in all the splendor around them. Christmas decorations abounded everywhere, and even though it was a holiday, the streets were crowded with tourists and locals alike.

"You should put your bag over your head," Clay said to Hayley as they walked along toward Rockefeller Center.

"What?" Hayley asked, stopping on the sidewalk. "Did you just tell me to put a bag over my head?"

"I meant your purse," Clay explained. "Don't just hang it on your shoulder like that. It's safer over your head."

"Sure sounded like he was telling you to cover your head up, Hayley." Emma laughed. "Maybe you should walk behind us, too."

"Dad, if you want, I can go back and wait in the car." Hayley grinned.

"You two are a riot," Clay added, walking on.

Emma took lots of photos everywhere they went, stopping at store window displays to take them in and to pose by the amazing tree at Rockefeller Center. She looked over the rink to see the many skaters below, thinking back to just a few days ago when she and Noah skated on Emerald Lake and what that led to for her.

The day passed rapidly with the sightseeing, and the trio stopped off for a nice meal at Mustang Harry's not far from Madison Square Garden.

"Dad, I don't think we can just walk in here and get a table, especially today," Emma warned.

"Don't worry," Clay told her. "It's all taken care of."

Clay entered and introduced himself, and they were led over to a booth reserved for them.

"When did you have time to arrange all this?" Emma wondered.

"Who cares?" Hayley answered as she looked around at the iconic Irish sports bar. "This place is great."

Emma dined on a fine meal, enjoying the roasted filet mignon baguette dripping with caramelized onions, brie, and horseradish cream. The three then made their way over to the Garden with full stomachs, where a long line of fans had already formed looking to get in to see Foo Fighters.

Once they got in through security, Emma was shocked when they were led to the area closest to the stage. She sat in awe, looking around at the immense crowd starting to fill the arena while Foo Fighters' songs blared over the speakers. She looked at the stagehands and security rushing around, moving items, speaking into headsets and walkie-talkies, trying to get the show underway.

With the space nearly at capacity, Emma sat down in her seat and placed her earplugs in, muffling some sounds around her.

"You're really going to wear those all night?" Hayley yelled to her.

"If it drowns out your singing, yes," she announced, noticing her father smiled.

The house lights started to go down, and the crowd erupted in a roar as the focus came to the stage.

A man dressed in a Santa Claus suit wandered out into the spotlight to the applause before picking up the microphone.

"I know you're all waiting for the Foos to come out, but before they take the stage, we have a special Christmas treat for you. Tonight's opening act is something different, a classic band from the beginnings of the Foo Fighters era. So let's give a big hand for Diagnosis!"

Santa Claus darted off the stage as Emma shot a look over at her father, who shrugged his shoulders as he clapped, adding to the polite applause coming from the crowd. Emma rose from her seat to see Noah walk out on stage and take his place at the piano practically in front of her. He didn't look down in her direction but instead started playing right away, diving into the first song as Ray belted out the words to "Coming Home," one of the songs from an early album that Emma had listened to.

The crowd was receptive to the first song, enjoying it before the band blew the doors off the place with three straight, proper rock songs. Emma found herself standing up, clapping, and singing along, and she noticed that more of the audience got into the music with each tune.

When the band finished playing "This Is Our House," another early favorite, Emma watched as Ray sat down on the stool at the center of the stage. The spotlight focused on him as he spoke.

"We only have two songs left for you before the real stars get out here," Ray announced, "so we want to do something special for you to close out our night as a way to say thanks and happy holidays."

Emma heard the familiar beginnings of the piano playing "The Christmas Song." She watched closely as Noah played, hoping he would turn in her direction to notice her, but he kept his attention rapt on the keys before him as Ray sang the tune. The crowd sang along with the music, and Emma saw that even her father and sister were singing now.

Once the Christmas tune was finished, Ray retook the spotlight.

"To close out the night, we have something brand-new for you. I know we would close out with one of our classic tunes, but this is a special occasion for us. So I'm going to turn things over to one of the founders of our band and our true leader, the man at the piano, Mr. Noah Healy."

The spotlight swung in Noah's direction and circled him. Noah pulled the microphone positioned on his piano closer to his lips. Emma pulled her earplugs out, hanging on every word he offered up.

"Thanks, Ray," Noah began. "Like Ray said, this is a special night for us. We haven't played in front of a crowd this big in a long time, and it's a treat for all of us, so thanks for letting us entertain you. Secondly, we have a new song for you. I haven't written anything new in a while, but lately, I've been feeling inspired. I just wrote this one, and I hope you like it. This one is for you, Emma."

Noah looked down in Emma's direction and smiled at her as he began to play lightly. Emma's heart leaped to her throat as she listened to the words he sang.

"All those years ago

I never gave much thought to us

Hanging out, being friends, having fun

For me was just a plus

When we met up years later,

Never thinking much about times past

I saw you in a new light

With feelings that came to last.

Now all that seems to pass us by

Were worlds apart again

And I don't know why.

All I can say is what's long overdue

For what it's worth, I love you too.

We came together, both lost souls

Trying to find a way to move on

Working to resolve pains of times of years ago

Never believing it was all forgone

Now all that seems to pass us by

We're worlds apart again

And I don't know why.

All I can say is what's long overdue

For what it's worth, I love you too

Even though we've drifted now

And still feel far apart

I need to let you know

How I feel deep in my heart.

And all I can say is what's long overdue

For what it's worth, I love you too.

The song ended with tears rolling down Emma's face. Noah had looked at her the entire time he sang, only looking away when the instrumental section of the love song came before the final verses. The crowd loved it and gave the band a massive ovation as they left the stage, causing the members to take several bows before they left.

Emma wiped at her face and found her hands shaking.

"Did you know he was going to do that?" Hayley shouted over the din to her sister. All Emma could do was shake her head.

"Did you, Dad?" Hayley asked, turning to their father.

"I may have heard a rumor about it," he answered coyly as Emma charged her father and gave him a hug.

"Is there any way we can go see him?" Emma asked excitedly.

Clay's face withdrew the smile he had.

"I tried really hard for that, honey. I truly did," Clay said solemnly. "There's too much security back there, and I couldn't do it. I'm sorry."

Emma nodded sadly. "It's okay. I'll always have this to remember."

Emma sat back in her seat, taking in the rest of the concert but not paying much attention to it. She put her earplugs back in when Foo Fighters came out and performed their songs, and it was everything the crowd wanted and more. Hayley was hoarse by the end of the night from yelling, screaming, and singing, while Emma had spent most of the set with her eyes closed, half-listening to Dave Grohl sing and the band play, and half of the time replaying Noah's song in her mind.

As Foo Fighters came out for their final encore, Dave Grohl stepped up to the mike and spoke. He thanked the crowd for all they had done, wished everyone a Merry Christmas, and thanked Diagnosis for coming in on short notice to open for them. He then pulled Noah out on stage to get him at the piano while the band went into their classic tune, "Everlong."

Emma saw how happy Noah looked in his true element, playing like the star he was on the stage. She smiled and even sang along to some of the words she could remember as Hayley put her arm around her to sing with her. Then, as the song ended and Noah finished playing with a strong flourish, he looked over and winked at Emma, and she broke into a gigantic smile.

The crowd slowly filtered out of the Garden as the house lights came back up, and Emma waited a bit, hoping that Noah might come out to see her. Then, unfortunately, security began to clear the inner area they sat in, and they had to leave. Hayley wrapped her arm around her sister and continued singing as they walked down the city streets, headed toward where they had parked the truck.

"That was incredible, Em! I've never experienced anything like that. Oh, Dave Grohl's voice makes me melt," she said, feigning a faint.

"It was nice," Emma said softly.

"Nice? Were we at the same show?" Hayley said, aghast. "It was way above nice, Emma! For crying out loud, you had someone sing a song to you from the stage at Madison Square Garden! Why aren't you doing cartwheels over this?"

"Oh, I am, believe me." Emma smiled, looking over at her father as she patted her chest.

18

The long drive home gave Emma plenty of opportunity to replay the moments of the night in her mind. She drifted off to sleep several times through the night, dreaming of different scenarios where she was up on stage with Noah or alone in the arena, with him singing to her and only her.

When Emma jolted awake as Clay pulled the truck in the driveway and stopped, she glanced at the clock on the dashboard and saw it was nearly four in the morning.

"You okay, Dad?" Emma yawned.

"Thank God for coffee," Clay admitted wearily as he climbed out of the truck. "Come on, Hayley, we're home," he said as he nudged Hayley awake in the back seat.

Hayley dragged herself out of the car, leaning on Emma as they both walked toward the front door and entered the house. Hayley trudged up the stairs, muttering, "Thank you, Daddy," as she moved to her room.

"Thank you, Dad," Emma said, choking up again. "It was the best Christmas present ever. I'll never forget it."

"You're welcome, princess," Clay answered, kissing his daughter on the forehead. "I'm going to bed. I have to get up for work in three hours." He smiled.

Emma walked to her room, pulled off her jeans, and climbed into bed, feeling almost energized now that she was home. However, she worried that going to sleep would make the entire day feel less authentic and wanted to hold onto it for as long as she could before she faded into slumber on her bed.

When Emma did awaken, it was nearly noon, and she jumped from the bed, worried she was late for something before realizing she had nothing to do today. There was no work to prepare for, all the holiday stuff was over, and she had nowhere she had to be.

Emma dressed and wandered from her room, stopping at Hayley's room but finding only Hayley's messed bed. When Emma went downstairs, she came across a note on the kitchen table from her mother, letting Emma know that she and Hayley had gone out to hit some after Christmas sales.

With nothing going on, Emma grabbed her hat and coat and went for a walk herself. The weather had warmed some more, allowing for more melting. The snow angels she and Noah had made were melded together into a giant blob on the lawn now. Emma made her way down to the Birch Tree and saw her father, bleary-eyed but still standing, at the counter helping customers. Emma pointed, asking if she should come in to assist him, but he waved her off, so she kept walking.

After passing the pub and diner, Emma realized she was closing in on the hotel. She hopped to the other side of the street instead of walking to the hotel entrance, not wanting to attract any attention from anyone. She made her way to the sidewalk that ran parallel to Emerald Lake, where a few kids were out skating and playing hockey.

Emma hummed along as she moved, finding she was humming the music to the song Noah had sung to her last night. Finally, she closed in on the Travers house at the end of the block and began to slow down as she neared the front of it. She stopped just short of the gate entrance and saw a real estate sign out front with a red banner across it that read "sale pending."

Emma's heart sank when she saw the posting. She glanced up the front steps to the porch and saw that the door to the house was wide-open. She gently opened the gate and climbed the front steps, feeling some weakness in the wood there as she moved before reaching the front door.

Emma stood in the doorway and peeked in, seeing nothing but empty space.

"Hello?" she said sheepishly.

When no one answered, she took a few further steps inside and looked around. Her boots echoed through each empty space as she looked at the fixtures hanging from the ceiling and all the delicate wood carvings she knew were there. Finally, Emma passed into the kitchen, swinging the door open, and saw that most kitchen fixtures had been removed, leaving her sad and wondering about the new owners' plans. She paced through the large kitchen before getting out and heading back to the winding staircase.

Emma still had seen no one inside and wondered who would leave the door open like this, assuming it must have been an oversight by the realtor. She entered the master bedroom upstairs, a room she recalled was beautifully decorated by Mrs. Travers but now stood empty. She moved to the immense walk-in closet, stepping inside and running her hand across the bare wood shelves.

It was then that Emma heard a faint sound coming from below. She froze in place, afraid that the new owner was indeed here and would discover her waltzing through their home uninvited. She hoped she could sneak out as quickly as she had slipped into the house and leave unnoticed.

Emma opened the bedroom door and stepped out, the floor creaking loudly beneath her. The noises were more significant when she reached the stairs, with each one groaning as she hit it. The noise became louder and more distinct now as if it were music playing from one of the rooms. When she reached the bottom of the steps and saw the coat rack by the door adorned with a red plaid jacket, she stopped.

Maybe someone working in here? Emma thought to herself as she moved to the door. Before she could step out, she stopped in her tracks when she heard the playing of "Over the Rainbow."

Emma went left and turned the corner into the large parlor room there, and stopped. She saw Noah, seated at a piano, playing the tune with his eyes closed. He opened his eyes and smiled when he spotted Emma.

"I was wondering if you might show up if you heard the right song." Noah smiled.

Emma darted over to Noah and hugged him tightly before grabbing his face and kissing him.

"What are you doing here?" She gasped.

"I heard you stopped by the show last night and wanted to see what you thought of it," he told her.

"It was—it was unbelievable," she whispered.

"I'm glad you liked it," Noah said as he rose from the piano bench. "Apparently, a lot of other people liked it too." Noah moved to one of the large windows that overlooked the side lawn.

"What do you mean?"

"Someone videoed the song and posted it online," Noah started. "I guess it went viral. You can thank your sister for that. Anyway, Jerry began to get calls last night about it right away. We have a few new record labels interested in picking us up, and I think I have some interviews I'll be doing, at least in a few days. For now, though, I have other things I need to do."

"Like what?" Emma asked as she approached Noah.

"Oh, that's right, I haven't had the chance to talk to you much, but now that the no contact order expired and you don't work at the hotel anymore—"

"Oh, you heard about that, huh?" Emma said, embarrassed.

"Your dad let me know, which I have to say, was more than a little awkward to talk about with him." Noah smiled. "Anyway, I should let you know that I've decided to get rid of my apartment in the city. I went there, and it was just too small, too dark, and... too lonely. So I got a different place—this place," he said, holding his hands out.

"What?"

"Yeah, you can thank your father for most of that, too. When he came down to see me, we worked it all out. He knew Mrs. Travers was getting ready to let this place go but hadn't put it on the market yet. When he told me that, I asked him to go to her, remind her about me, and tell her I wanted to buy it—for you."

Emma stood in awe, unsure of how to respond. "Noah, what are you talking about—"

Noah interrupted Emma right away.

"Emma, in my heart, I think I always knew Emerald Lake was the one place that felt like home to me. I always felt welcome years ago, and that hadn't changed when I came back. So when I saw you and spent time with you like I did, I knew it for sure. Just spending those few days with you, and then without you, convinced me. You wanted this place, I wanted to come here, and I needed you. We can make all that happen."

Noah picked up a rectangular box in the corner and handed it to Emma.

"Open it," he bade.

Emma put the box down on the piano bench and lifted the top off. Inside was a wood-carved sign.

"Believe Inn Bed&Breakfast," she read before turning back to Noah.

"I know it will take some work and time," Noah said as he took Emma's hand, "but I think if we get people in here, maybe we can be open for Fourth of July, just in time for fireworks over the lake. The guys in the band have agreed to work with me on my schedule so I can be here with you instead of on the road as much."

Emma let go of Noah's hand and walked out to the center of the room, looking around before she pivoted back and faced Noah.

"So, what do you say?" Noah asked.

"This is all so fast. It doesn't even seem possible," Emma said in disbelief. "Is this real?"

Noah stepped to Emma and wrapped his arms around her before kissing her.

"I can pinch you if you'd like me to convince you it's real," he whispered to her.

"You wrote a song," Emma said joyfully, "and then you came back, and then this—for me?"

"Yes, for you," Noah said, looking into Emma's brown eyes. "I love you, Emma, and I don't want that to slip away from me again."

Noah caressed Emma's cheek with the back of his hand before kissing her again.

"For what it's worth, I love you too," she whispered back.